As We Ride, We Die 3:

Friendz to the End

L. Triplett

Prologue

Pandemonium....

The funeral, itself, was a burial. Heavenly Pearly Gates Baptist
Church was brimming over with Death's angels as people begged Ebony
to stop. In her hands, she held a fully loaded Glock 40 caliber pistol.
Other than the frightening sight of her trembling hands and smeared
mascara, she seemed focused and determined to complete her mission.

"Safari Malice, you murdering bastard! You killed Tahja! You
killed Taj!" Ebony screamed. Nothing about her appearance was able to
mask the pain or hatred in her heart. The tears and unsteady aim spoke
what words didn't.

Not accustomed to such a display at a funeral, the congregation
of family and friends were stricken with silence and motionless. It was
Ebony's screaming that brought Willo out of the trance. Him and his
partner Mainlife sprung into action in the nick of time.

Blah!

"Ebony," Stunna yelled in disbelief.

The sound of the gunshot disrupted the quietness within the
church's reception area. The recoil sent a shockwave up Ebony's arms.
Her firm grip around the pistol loosened as it jerked her aim upward.
The echoing of the shot brought back a sense of reality in Heavenly
Pearly Gates. Men and women of all ages screamed from fright, running
and hiding behind anything they felt to provide safety.

1

"Ahhh! I've been shot!" One of the ushers yelled, laying on the floor holding his right thigh.

Mainlife rushed over to assess the gunshot wound. Seeing the gaping hole through the pants leg, he sighed. "Bro, you'll be alright. It is a clean shot."

The usher's eyes widened, revealing the confused thoughts he was having about Mainlife's assessment. "What do you mean, I'll be alright? Can't you see that I have a hole in my leg, and it's pouring blood?"

"Listen, my nigga, the bullet went straight through. It ain't stuck in a bone or muscle. Count your fucking blessings." Mainlife replied, being irritated by the man's fear. "But if it'll make you feel better, I'll get someone to call an ambulance for your scary ass." He walked off without waiting for the usher's response.

Ebony was an emotional wreck. Tears streamed from her eyes like a waterfall while snot oozed from her nose. The gun slipped from her grip to the dark grey carpeted floor.

Blah!

The Glock went off on contact. Ebony's body shook violently. Her hate had overrid her moral judgement. She wasn't a killer at heart; however, she wasn't a pushover either. Especially when it came to someone messing with her heart, and that's what Safari Malice had done in her mind.

The bullet ricocheted off a highly polished brass flowerpot before being lodged in the wooden doorframe. The pastor's facial expression was one of disbelief. Without alarming anyone of his action, he scrammed,heading for the nearest phone to call the police. In everyone else's eyes, he looked to be running for his life.

James exited the restroom unaware of the drama that was in full effect. With people running around, screaming hysterically, it didn't take long for what was going on to resonate. He stood in front of the bathroom door doing his best to fend off the state of shock that was trying to claim his mind. Calming down, he scanned the area, looking for Willo.

"Uuuughhh.... Get off of me!" Ebony demanded. Stunna had wrapped her up in a bear hug, and taken her down to the floor.

"Just chill, Ebony," Stunna said as calmly as the situation would allow.

Security guards came flooding into the reception area. Stunna had Ebony restrained, but he was also choking her until being kicked in the side by one of the guards.

"Nigga, you tripping," Mainlife yelled as he left Willo behind the beam they'd taken cover behind.

"Get up, bro," Sqizzle shouted, shoving one of the ushers out of his way.

The sound of sirens echoed within the building. Before anyone could react, the city police came barging in, knocking the sliding glass door off track.

"Mr. Malone," James screamed while making his way through the chaos. The security guards restrained Ebony. "We gotta go!" He'd reached Willo, and ushered him out of the place.

"Where's my baby?! Andrew! Andrew! Where's my baby?!" Linda screamed while running out of the church with Cynthia hot on her heels.

Chapter One

"Jo... Ebony was bugging, calling bro Safari Malice. Where the hell she get that from? Why the fuck was she even there?" Mainlife said. He'd returned to Willo's bedside in the hospital with snacks.

Stunna and Sqizzle were watching a BET movie in the presence of a sleeping Willo. Mainlife tossed them Sprite sodas and bags of Doritos. He, himself, plopped down into the chair, where his suit jacket hung over.

"Thanks bro. I don't know why she was there. T-La was talking bout a Safari Malice last week." Stunna said.

"Gotta be the same nigga then. That's the first time I heard the nigga name." Sqizzle said. He untwisted the cap off the Sprite, and chugged half the drink.

"Why the fuck she screaming his name? Who dude is?" Mainlife asked as he strolled through the contacts on his Galaxy S10 phone.

"From what the streets say, the nigga who robbed Doug Jones." Sqizzle replied in between wolfing down Doritos. "Where ol girl from anyway?"

"Shawty I snagged on the Westside on that Malcolm wild goose chase." Stunna said as he stood up and stretched.

"Robbed Doug Jones? Man, get the fuck outta here. You ain't gonna convince me the infamous Doug Jones went out like a sack." Mainlife said, smashing the last of the Sour Cream and Onions Chips.

"The words of that nigga he slide with, T-La, yup. Ya boy went out like a sack." Sqizzle replied.

The room door opened. Mainlife, Stunna and Sqizzle ended their conversation as James walked in, carrying a tray. "Alright, visiting hours are over. Y'all can leave now. I got it from here. Besides, I'm working a double shift tonight."

"Bro, fuck what you saying. We ain't leaving the homie up in here by himself." Mainlife interjected.

James sighed. "Young man, we've all had a long day. It's by God's grace he's still alive and breathing on his own. The same could be said about every last one of you. Is being in the streets, making fast money, living the hood dreams worth dying for?"

"Whatever, man. Let's bounce." Mainlife said. Stunna and Sqizzle jumped out of the chairs and walked pass James, mugging him. "Don't get the hospital burnt down." Was the last thing Mainlife said before leaving out of the room.

The trio walked to the exit, planning their next move along the way. As they approached the automatic sliding doors that led to the parking garage, Mainlife unbuttoned his shirt. He bee lined to the gloss bowling ball blue Regal, sitting on reverse eights. He hopped in the driver's seat, and tossed the shirt on the passenger's side before starting the engine.

Stunna and Sqizzle was in the cocaine white Cutlass still lost for words. Finally, Stunna mashed the gas, trailing Mainlife through and out of the parking garage. Driving through Grady Homes, both cars were gripping the asphalt hard. Although it was night, people were staring from every angle as they raced by.

***

After leaving Burger King's drive thru, Ice drove into traffic in deep thought. He was finding it hard to digest the fact of having gone on a wild goose chase. The mission he'd gone on ended up being a waste of his time and a free murder case if he'd been caught. Taking the advice of a fiend name Leroy, the dream of hitting a major score was all he wanted.

The come up. A fast come up to change the game's field for me. He thought to himself. But, instead of a nice heist, he'd found Safari Malice, brutalized.

Ice hated the fact he'd exposed his hand for nothing. His whole crew was mad. Even the two new recruits were expressing their dislike of the situation. It was like playing Russian Roulette with a semiautomatic, a no win situation.

From his childhood friend, Dig, on down, Ice had built a team. Blot and Juice trained the two new recruits, Hot and Man, sealing the five man goon squad. Coming up on his cousin's house, Ice was prioritizing his next steps. He knew he couldn't or wasn't about to go out bad.

Pulling up in the subdivision, he smiled, remembering the mind your own business policy the community stood on. The street lights washed over the townhouses with its orange hue. Ice steered the Ford F-150 to the bottom of the horseshoe. Clutching the cold blue steel, he surveyed the area before getting out of the truck.

***

Pulling up at the trap on Grant Street, Mainlife and Stunna spotted a navy blue Lincoln Town Car parked on the curb. Grant Street was always alive. Hustlers were posted, handling the gas flow of traffic, serving the occupants of every vehicle like a drive thru under the blood moon. Mainlife and Stunna parked out front of an abandoned house across the street from the trap house.

As they got out of the Regal, Mainlife's Scratch ringtone went off. After looking at the caller ID, he motioned for Stunna and Sqizzle to go on over. Once they'd crossed the street, he answered the phone. "What up, ma?"

"You know what's up. I need to re-up." The woman replied.

Mainlife checked the time on his Citizen Eco-Drive watch. It was 8:26pm. "Alright. You gotta give me a minute."

"My nigga, minutes without work, are uncounted for dollars. Don't keep me waiting too long." She shot back.

He couldn't argue with that. "How much you trying to cop, ma?"

"The usual, plus a half."

"Damn.... You stepping your game up. I like that."

The woman laughed. "Whatever, nigga. Don't let me find out."

"Find out what?" The answer to Mainlife's question was a disconnected call. As he walked across the street, a candy apple red Acura Legend sped by him. The driver blew the horn and waved at him. "Crazy bitch."

***

After knocking three times on the double steel plated door, Dig opened it to find Ice standing with a Burger King carryout bag.

"What's good, Dig? You get up with them niggas Blot and Juice?" Asked Ice.

"Not yet," answered Dig.

"You slipping, fam. Where you think them fools at?" Ice said, standing his 6'4 and 240 pounds frame in front of Dig.

Dig shrugged his shoulders. "The hell if I know. I hope you ain't got no onions on the burgers this time."

"If it is, pick the shit off. Huh." Ice shoved the carryout bag at Dig, before walking around him, heading for the kitchen.

"Damn, nigga. Oh E. T. phone home looking ass boy. I'm gonna take ya ass out, Willie B twin face ass. I don't know why you got a tattoo on ya creepy crawler face ass." Dig jonesed while unwrapping a burger.

Ice paid him no mind. The smirk on his face was for his cousin. Her face was buried in a book of natural remedies for humans.

"Hey man, you got onions on here!" Dig yelled.

"So! Just like I said, pick it off!" Ice shouted back, waking his cousin from her sleep.

"Why y'all niggas always gotta be so loud? What time is it?" She said in between yawns.

"Damn... My bad, cuz." Ice apologized.

"Danielle, this nigga keep fucking up orders. He got onions on the burgers again." Dig complained as he walked in the kitchen. He tossed the bag on the table, keeping three burgers for himself. Ice didn't even care to comment.

"Anyway, Dee, it's time to handle that situation while you still in ya uniform." Ice said as she stretched and wiped the cold from her eyes.

"Give me a sec," Danielle managed to say while yawning.

"Alright. We will be in the basement. Come on down when you ready."

Dig, picking the onions off the burger, flicking them on the back of Ice's shirt, followed him through the house. He was three inches shorter than Ice, and all he ever did was, talk trash to his cousin. Ice ignored him, focusing his attention on the task at hand. They entered the basement to find their captive propped up against the far wall.

Ice walked across the concrete floor to stand, towering over Safari Malice. "Dig, shut the fuck up. Know the difference in a time for bullshitting and the time for playing for keeps." He had grown tired of ignoring the comical rants coming from his cousin.

Blood Moon

Chapter Two

The interior light of the Lincoln Town Car came on when the driver opened the door. A cloud of smoke accompanied the baldheaded dark brown skin man who got out upon watching Stunna approach through the rearview mirror.

"Who you looking for?" Stunna asked without getting into formalities. He stood toe to toe with the man. Sqizzle was to his left, and a group of young hustlers were behind them, expressing their dislike for strangers by pulling and aiming guns at the baldheaded man who continued to smoke the Black and Mild cigar.

"You better not be the nigga Dan talking bout," Sqizzle said, warningly as they searched him at gunpoint.

Fifty hands and feet were on the man before he knew it. The pavement welcomed him face down as they brutally assaulted him.

"Who sent you," Stunna screamed while steadily kicking the screaming man in the ribs.

The commotion caught Mainlife's attention real quick. "What the fuck?!" He ran headfirst in the midst with the nickel plated Bulldog 44 held down at his side. He came to the clearing in the middle just in time, shining the phone's flashlight on the scene to see Stunna doing the A-Town Stomp on the man's head like it was a cockroach.

"Whoa! Y'all niggas pump ya brakes! Back the fuck up!" Mainlife demanded, having to shove Stunna off the man.

"You know this nigga," asked Stunna, smoothing his shirt down.

"Yeah. This my mans and them, Stew." Mainlife replied. He looked down at him, shaking his head. "Damn, old school, you was bout to make the missing person's ads. Not to mention, your ass made the news. What the fuck happened?"

Stunna apologized, but the old school hustler waved it off. "Y'all good, youngsters. I respect the game. You gotta protect ya turf. Besides, I thought my man Mainlife saw me when he rolled up."

"My fault. My thoughts were somewhere else. Just got back from a funeral. Why you cut ya hair?" Mainlife said while he helped Stew clean himself up.

"Fox 5," he replied.

"Fox 5 what?"

"News, nigga."

Mainlife smirked. "Since when the news make you cut your hair?"

"Since you," Stew shot back.

"Hold up. What the hell you niggas got going on?" Stunna said after half listening to their conversation.

Stew nodded towards Mainlife. "Ya people know. It's called capitalism. Too much unaccounted for money, somebody gotta answer for it."

"Yeah, that's out of my league. I'll holla." Stunna said and stepped off, followed by Sqizzle and the others.

Mainlife waited to they were out of earshot before addressing the situation. "What we looking at?"

"About....," Stew paused and stared at the black Ford Taurus as it crept by at a cruise speed. Mainlife's attention was drawn to the same vehicle with the mirror tinted windows.

"Say bruh, let's go inside the spot. Get you a drink to ease ya pain." Mainlife said in an uneasy tone while staring at the taillights of the Ford Taurus.

"My man, you must be a mind reader. Let's do it."

They walked inside the trap house and bypassed everyone, heading for the kitchen. Stew sat at the dining table while Mainlife grabbed two shot glasses, a fifth of Paul Mason and two Natural Ice beers.

"That's the fourth time that Ford Taurus rode through here. Capitalism, my ass. Atlanta is top ten. I'm out. Chi-town me. Be safe and sound out here, my nigga." Stew said after he downed the third shot of Paul Mason.

"I feel that, bruh. Hold it down." Mainlife replied. They sat and talked money and politics while finishing off the fifth of liquor and their beers. After the bottles were bone dry, Stew pounded Mainlife up, and made his way out.

Mainlife and Stunna stood in the doorway, watching Stew speed down Grant Street. Once the car was out of sight, they walked back into the living room.

"Flip the news on. Let me see what Stew talking bout." Mainlife said.

"Nigga, you know. I be back." Stunna replied, tossing him the television's remote.

"Where you headed?"

"Peep the scene and change clothes. Let Sqizz know."

"Yeah, alright. Just keep ya phone on. We gon' fuck around an double up on your ass."

"We ain't even gonna play them kinda games, my nigga."

"Play with it, and find out. Matter of fact, take one of them Gremlins with ya." Mainlife demanded.

Stunna ignored him, leaving out with a smirk on his face.

Stew's sudden appearance and comment had Mainlife in deep thought. He grabbed another beer from the refrigerator, and sat down at the kitchen table. Before popping the top, he took out his personal stash of marijuana, and twisted a fat blunt.

***

Danielle came in with the first aid kit, pushing Ice and Dig out of her way in order to get to the patient. Hating the task at hand, she did her best to hold her composure with Ice and Dig watching close by.

"They like that new dope I copped from Loco. It's been on point lately." Ice said, pulling a Newport Long from the pack.

"You ain't lying, but I ain't with riding all the way to Macon and back for the shit. That nigga be taxing." Dig commented. He cringed from the sight of Safari Malice's gaping wounds.

"Can't beat the ticket though. He got great numbers, and he fronted three off the rip."

"I get what you saying, but I'm gonna leave that trip up to you and Blot."

Ice nodded, taking a drag of the Newport while keeping a watchful eye on Safari Malice. *If you flinch wrong, I'm finishing the job someone else started, nigga.* He thought. His phone began vibrating against his right hip. "Yo. Hot and Man should be on the way for two pounds. I got em ready, next to Gucci bag." He ended the call, and placed the phone back in his pocket.

"You want me to serve em?" Asked Dig.

"Do what you do. I gotta watch this. Don't forget to stash the Gucci bag. Danielle will flip if she all that shit in here. It's gonna be a long night, but this is the last time we moving this nigga." Ice said.

"Bet. I told you to leave the nigga in the first place. I'm surprised he still breathing."

"Some niggas got a strong will to live. Anyway, they'll be here bout ten minutes." Ice reminded his cousin. He kept his eyes glued on Danielle, who was kneeling next to Safari Malice, feeding him. Dig trotted up the basement stairs, leaving them to patch him up.

Ice tapped the ashes from the cigarette while staring at Safari's battered body and scarred face. Danielle held a cup of Ensure with a straw in it up to his quivering lips. She was praying silently and fighting back the tears. She knew she needed to find a better way to feed the man, but she also knew her cousin was going to downplay any idea she thought of at the moment.

"Danielle, that's enough... I'm not trying to be down here all night. Finish changing the bandages, so you can be on your way to work." Ice said in the midst of exhaling a cloud of smoke. He thumped the Newport duck to the floor and smothered it out under the weight of his low cut hard bottom casual Timberland's.

Danielle was hesitant, putting the cup down. Safari Malice looked like a Fright Night Zombie. Picking up some gauzes out of the first aid kit, her stomach turned from the stench of dried blood and dead skin around the wounds and stuck to the old bandages. She choked down the vomit that was trying to come up.

There she was, trying to make some extra money, outside of her nursing career at Emory Memorial Hospital, and her side job as a dancer at The Blue Flame Gentlemen's Club. *It's always some extra shit with these niggas, Danielle mumbled under her breath.* She hated having to do what she took pride in for her little cousin, Ice. She poured rubbing alcohol and peroxide onto his wounds and soaked the gauzes in a mixture of it.

"Hsss...." Safari Malice winced. He was in excruciating pain. Beads of sweat popped up instantly on his forehead.

"Ice, I can't keep doing this shit." Danielle said. Between the stench and the inadequacy of the service she was performing, she didn't know which reason to lean on to support her argument.

"Come on, Dee. You know how it is out here; it's play for keeps. I'm pretty sure, you see worse shit than this come through the ER." Ice replied. Which was true. Young and old was brought through the emergency room door in droves when there's heat in the streets. Some with missing or dangling limbs.

"What the fuck, Ice? Dude's missing a fucking thumb. Whoever it was, they chopped off his thumb. Whatever he did, he didn't deserve this shit." She shot back coldly.

"You might be right, cuz. But the nigga thumb got cut off for a reason, and I wanna know why."

Safari Malice squirmed and hissed from the burning sensation caused by the alcohol and peroxide. Ice stood, breath hot on Danielle's neck, looking at him without caring for his condition.

Chapter Three

Ice's breath on the nape of her neck, and Safari's expression at the touch of the gauzes, had Danielle feeling uneasy. "You must like going through this shit?" She said as she finished stitching up the deep wound on his chest.

"Who are you referring to, cuz, me or him?" Asked Ice.

"You, nigga."

"Nah Dee, I don't. Let alone, having you patch up problems. But this is how a nigga eat.

"Don't think your looks give you a free meal ticket of living. It's more than looks. But, you know that...Because you keep bailing ya crackhead ass nigga out of jail. Don't take it personal. I'm just keeping it real,cuz. I'm helping both of us. We all we got."

"I can't keep doing this, Ice." Danielle sat sorting through the First Aid box,shaking her head as Safari Malice continued grunting.

"We won't. I promise....Step aside, Dee. Wat's ya name?" Ice demanded as Safari Malice hissing stopped.

"He's not in no condition to talk, Ice. Look at him! He barely looking at you."

Safari Malice lips parted as he slighty turned his head towards Ice.

"I need to know something, now. I'm not no Captain Save a Nigga! He owe me!" Ice said, leaning towards Safari Malice's face.

" Ice! Stop! Wait until he heal some."

" I don't got time for dat!"

"Wait to he heal." Danielle said, standing up over Ice with smeared blood on her uniform.

" Watch out, Dee! Wat's your name?" Ice said, moving Danielle out the way as he pulled the gun from his waiste line and centered it on Safari Malice's forehead.

Safari Malice's lips trembled as he tried to speak. Danielle looked on, terrified, as Ice gritted his teeth and pressed the gun harder against his skull.

***

" How you doing, Stunna? You called right on time. I'm still looking into that info for ya. I'm riding back from Tennessee. Is Willo good?"

"Yea, he good...Cokizzy.Shit got shell afta you left.I need dat info like yesterday." Stunna said as a U-Haul truck raced down the street with one tail light. He locked the house door and walked to the car.

" I'm on it...Move your hand giirrlll!"Cokizzy said with an attitude.

"Cokizzy...You straight?"Stunna said gassing the Cutlass to 60 miles ,racing down Milton Avenue.

" Why! You haven't call me, Stunna!" Yelled a woman.

"Get out the way, Alicia.Stunna, Ima get back at you." Cokizzy said ending the call.

Stunna heard Alilcia's voice loud and clear and stepped on the gas pedal harder.Stunna viewed the upcoming train tracks and eased up on the acceleration, looking both ways before crossing.

***

"Fuck! The Yang...had another camera!" Mainlife yelled, jumping up in disbelief, steady watching Fox 5 breaking news. Looking at the blurry glimpse, he knew it was him, pointing the gun as Stew stood behind him with his head down. He couldn't help but smirk, reaching in his pocket as he heard Sqizzle coming in the back door.

***

"Watch out, Dee!" Ice yelled.

"No! Ice! Stop!" Danielle screamed. Avoiding her cousin's stiff arm, she tripped on the first aid kit box. Safari Malice managed to open his left eye halfway.

"What's your name?" Asked Ice. The response he received was a groan of anguish and pain.

"Ice, go head on with your bullshit. Can't you see that he ain't in no condition for your q and a?"

Ice turned his attention to her. "Go upstairs, Dee. You done yo part. The rest is on me." Feeling her gentle, pleading touch on his elbow caused him to flinch. Not willing to give in to her demands, he brushed his cousin's hand away and pushed pass her.

Boc! Boc! Boc!

Danielle froze in place upon hearing the gunshots. Her cousin spun around with searching eyes. "Stay down here. I'll be back." She nodded, and watched as he ran up the stairs with the gun in his left hand. Safari Malice groaned, bringing her back to reality.

Quickly, Danielle grabbed hold of the mattress he laid on and, with determination, she pulled it in the additional room, and locked the door behind her. The sounds of the different caliber guns echoed throughout the basement. Safari Malice groaned from the pain he felt after rolling off the mattress onto the open nub of the cut off thumb.

"Shh... Be quiet before you get us killed." Danielle whispered. She rolled him back on the mattress, and laid down next to him. Every time a shot rang out, he felt the jolt of her body and could faintly hear her heart beating.

"What, nigga! You thought I was a sweet lick, nigga?! You should've known it'd be consequences fucking with a jack boy!" Another gunshot rang out. Danielle knew it wasn't either of her cousin's voices she'd heard, so she already expected the worst had happened.

Sensing and knowing her fear, Safari shielded her as best he could.

***

"Aye! Yo, Sqizz!"

"What up, bro?" Sqizzle yelled back as his musclebound Blue Star Pitbull Kujo came running in the kitchen. The dog was always energetic and slinging drool everywhere with his tongue dangling.

"You wanna try to get some get back on NBA Live, nigga?!"

"Yeah! Nigga, we betting a hun don every quarter! Sheba!" Sqizz replied. He yelled for his female Red Nose Pitbull that came racing into the kitchen and sat near his feet. "Damn, she quick."

Mainlife appeared in the kitchen doorway and squatted. "Kujo! Come here boy." Kujo trotted over to him. "Good boy." He stood up straight, walked on in, and sat at the table. "So, I did some homework. We have Safari Malice on one hand, and Malcolm Vic on the other."

"What Safari Malice do?"

Mainlife shrugged his shoulders. "Shit really. Besides, being the reason Ebony shot Willo."

"Hold up, bro... You know, shawty was on some psyched out shit. She said Safari killed Taj or Tahja. Some shit like that." Sqizzle said while walking out of the kitchen into the living room with Mainlife behind him.

"Sqizz, you high?"

"Nah. Why? What's the move?"

Mainlife tossed him the wireless PlayStation controller, before picking up the one sitting on the coffee table in front of him. "Nigga, you know what's up. Bout to get that mouth and money out ya."

"For real...."

For Mainlife, the game was a way to put his thoughts in perspective. Ever since the run-in with Stew, he'd been treading lightly, not knowing the real ins and outs of the situation. NBA Live 07 flared across the television screen, and both men smiled.

Mainlife bobbed his head to the background music while modifying his team's jersey for the playoff league at the United Center he'd created.

22

Bad News

Chapter Four

Night was upon them. Danielle's body ached, heart pounded and mind wondered to the thought of what might come. Safari Malice continued to give her as much comfort as his condition would allow. She allowed her body to concede to the comfort of his fearlessness, while listening to the voices of the unknown and the sound of moving furniture.

"Let's check the basement, Rack." Hot suggested.

"Nah, dawg, we out. Take the Gucci bag, and head to the car." Commanded Rack. He stood in the middle of the living room, looking down at Ice's bullet hole riddled body. He laid the sawed off pistol grip pump on the coffee table before taking the .357 short barrel out. Without hesitation, he squeezed the trigger three times, putting one between Ice's eyes and two in his chest. With the mission completed, in his mind, Rack ran out of the house, his long dreds shielding his face from the sight of any possible witnesses.

Danielle got up and moved with caution towards the stairwell. After waiting and listening to hear if anyone had stayed behind, she eased her way up the stairs. In the light, the bloodstains on her uniform was more than enough to remind her of the kind of day she'd had. Her house had been a warzone, which was unsuspected.

"Ice," she whispered, nearing the top of the stairs. Her fear made the twelve stairs seem like thirty. There wasn't a reply. The strong scent of gunpowder and death lingered in the air.

As she entered the kitchen, she spotted Dig's blue and black Bo Jackson's sneakers toes pointed to the ceiling. "Dig?" She whispered between quivering lips. Goosebumps covered her body, expecting the worst as she looked around the corner.

Bullet holes were everywhere she turned - the television, picture frames, everything was a reminder of what had happened. "Dig! No..." Danielle's hands trembled. Her body went numb at the sight of Dig's bloody body.

"Dee...." She heard her name spoken faintly. Immediately, she left one painstaking scene to visit another. Upon reaching Ice, her mind went blank, seeing the blood oozing from the bullet hole in the side of his face.

"Ice.... Why God?" Danielle was destraught. She dropped to her knees next to her cousin's body. The blood that pooled around his body soaked into the knee padding of the shrubs she wore.

She started pounding on his chest, screaming at the top of her lungs. Her pain filled screams traveled through the night. So caught up in her emotions, she hadn't heard the footsteps storming through the house.

    ***

"Baauuun! I Boozer ya ass, nigga! I told you, Benny gon get that ass wrapped tonight! Shit ain't 96."

"Watch ya mouth with them chicken nuggets. I live to pluck feathers."

"Tighten up on the bet then," Sqizzle said, sitting the joystick on the coffee table. He reached in his pocket, pulled out a wad of cash, and counted two hundred off. "Add two hundred more to the pot, my nigga." He tossed the money on the pile already on the coffee table.

"Oh, shit!" Mainlife shouted, jumping up off the couch. Acouple of high beaming headlights flashed through the front window.

***

"Danielle, what the fuck? Blot yelled. He ran to her side, looking like a knockoff Wesley Snipes. Juice followed close behind, looking like T.I. with tattoos all in his face.

"Dammit man," Juice said, shaking his head as he surveyed the scene. It had been a bloodbath. "I'm gon go check the rest of the house." He hurried off with his gun at the ready if necessary, but his years of experience was telling him all the damage had been done, and the people responsible were long gone.

"Who did this, Danielle?" Blot shouted, holding her close to him. Her bloody hands shook violently. It was clear to him that she was fighting going into shock.

Dig's, riddled with bullet holes, body had Juice doubling back to the bathroom. He'd seen enough. All he wanted was blood for blood now.

"Speed shit up, Juice! We gotta get Dee outta here!" Blot yelled, lifting Danielle out of the puddle of blood.

***

"Mal... Malice.. Malll... Malcolm... Tasha... Tahja... Sha.. Ja.. Taj.. Damn! Ain't this some shit? Shorty and dude must've been fucking around."

"So, you high now? Nigga, press play." Sqizzle said, exhaling the Chronic smoke.

"On some real nigga shit, we been chasing ghosts. When we was on the westside, them hoes and niggas was stressing the names Mal and Taj. This nigga, Safari Malice, he's the one who been busting at Willo." Mainlife replied, pulling out his phone.

"He killed Mollie," Sqizzle yelled, jumping to his feet. The marijuana smoke made him choke due to his fast movement.

"We gotta change clothes... Hit Alfred. Tell him to hold the spot down. Sheba! Kujo! Let's go." Mainlife commanded.

Sqizzle left out the house with his mind in a dark place. Death was the leading thought, and there was several images appearing, disappearing, and reappearing in his mind's sight on how to make it happen. Spotting Alfred on the corner of Nolan, he got his attention before calling Stunna.

***

"Where Danielle," Juice asked with a distasteful look on his face.

"She's in the car. We gotta move this nigga from the basement." Blot said.

"Man, fuck that nigga! The dope gone. Ain't shit in this bitch. Niggas hit em for everything."

"Bruh, bring yo ass on."

"I been told Ice to ditch that nigga. Now look - him and Dig dead."

"Nigga, I can see."

"Bet the shit right up your alley."

"What? Juice, you tripping my nigga." Blot spoke in a tone, letting Juice know he was pushing it. He trotted down the basement's stairs, with Juice hot on his heels.

"Nah, I ain't tripping," Juice shot back in a hushed tone as they descended the stairs.

***

Stunna ended the call, leaving Sqizzle in serious thought while cruising down Pryor Road. Traffic was at an all time minimum, making it easy for him to observe his surroundings and handle the Cutlass at the same time. While the phone rang in his ear, he kept close attention on the headlights beaming through the rearview mirror.

"What up, Napoleon? How're you doing?"

"I'm good, Peach. Where Moll Moll?" Stunna replied, eyeing the black minivan that pulled alongside of the Cutlass, swerving.

Change Of Plan

Chapter Five

"Napoleon, you alright," Peach yelled through the receiver. Everything had gone silent on Stunna's end.

"Yeah," he replied,, still looking at the minivan.

"OK. Moll Moll in the back, sleeping."

"Cool. Can you get somebody to watch him? I need you to check something out with me."

Peach looked at the time. "It's late."

"I know, but it's beneficial."

"I don't know if Lisa's up."

"Go check an see. I'm headed your way now."

"Dammit man. I wish you would've hit my line earlier. You know how I hate this short notice shit."

"Who the fuck is this," Stunna said, irritated. He honked his horn twice. The minivan was too close for comfort.

"Are you sure you good?"

"I'm good, Peach. Call Lisa." He repeated as he leaned back in the seat and fingered the trigger of the MACK 11.

***

Police cruisers were parked everywhere in the subdivision where Danielle lived. Detectives were patrolling from house to house, searching for any possible lede to help put an end to the double homicide. For the most part, they were at dead ends - nobody spoke a word of what was heard or seen if they had witnessed it. While comparing notes, the detectives stood shaking their heads more out of frustration than disbelief.

Blot sat comforting Danielle in her Ford Focus. She was hunched over, crying as her house was being taped off and searched. Rubbing her back, he kept his eyes on the police. Being in close proximity with the cops always gave him butterflies.

Watching from the dead end of the subdivision parked in front of Danielle's neighbor's house, Blot noticed no lights were on. He shook his head at the thought of the lack of concern for the lives of young black men. *Just two more dead niggas in their eyes,* he thought to himself.

***

The minivan passenger's side window was rolled down, and the passenger stuck his head and left arm out the window, motioning for Stunna to pullover. As the traffic light turned red, Stunna pulled into the parking lot and around to the side of a BP gas station.

"Nigga, you almost got yo ass blasted, pulling up on me like that, Abe," Stunna said, holding up the MACK 11.

"Man, ain't nobody trying to hear that shit. We been tried flagging your ass down in front of South Side Clinic." Abe shot back.

"Bruh, I'm on the move. Who driving?" Stunna wanted to know.

"Bear."

"Ah hell. What up, Woog?!"

"What's up, Stunna," Bear replied, leaning forward in the seat so he could see him. "Bruh, you ever catch up with that Malcolm fool?"

Stunna shook his head. "Hell nah. But lil bruh just hit me up with some crazy shit. Nigga name Safari Malice. Y'all ever heard of the nigga?"

"I haven't," said Abe.

"Nah... I can't recall. But, Q-Ball and Blood been running up on them east side niggas bout Malcolm. They been lighting Glenwood up." Bear said.

"That's what's up. Bro, y'all niggas stay in tune."

"Alright, Stunna. My mom's still talking bout you."

"Abe, you know Officer David some bullshit. He's crooked as fuck. Y'all be safe." Stunna pulled off and made a left on Ralph D. Abernathy as Bear steered off to the right, heading in the direction of Turner Field.

Stunna drove in silence, maintaining his observation - thanks to Bear and Abe's news. Making a right turn on McDaniel Street, he was prepared for the usual lively atmosphere of the notorious redbrick projects better known as Mechanicsville by its occupants. He steered the Cutlass with one hand with the other on the trigger as he moved in the direction of Peach's apartment. *Welcome to the concrete jungle,* he thought to himself, turning into the parking space in front of her residence.

Stunna automatically spotted the group of men, dressed in all black hoodies, standing under the streetlight. Mechanicsville had a story of its own. He dialed Peach's number again. "I'm outside, Peach." He ended the call without hearing a reply.

He allowed his eyes to drift towards the adjacent apartment complex at a, what looked like, a drama scene about to unfold. Three women and a pimp, who wore a lime green three piece suit with the top hat to match, were arguing about payment. Other than that, it was the regular going on around him - dope was being sold, and the fiends were partying hard in the gangways, paranoid throughout the night.

Still observing the scenes about him, Stunna managed to let his thoughts flow. As he waited on Peach, he began reminiscing on Mainlife's question he'd asked at the funeral.

"You told her?"

Thinking Ebony was a stalker, he'd scratched her off his mental as things started to add up. One of Mollie's favorite lines came to him as a reminder. *"Neph, everything happens for a reason. Trust me on that, Napoleon."* Stunna nodded, appreciating the words - more now than ever.

"Bitch! Who in the hell do you take me for?" The words of the outraged pimp brought Stunna back to reality just in time to see him backhand one of the women across the right side of her face.

***

Choke sat with Clever, enjoying his wealthy lifestyle. He was eating like an Italian in his upscale palace in King's Point on Dunwoody.

"I told you, he'll take care of it. This what he do... Pass the cocktail sauce and garlic butter." Choke said between chews to his bilingual Hispanic maid.

Clever half listened, sipping champagne with little nods of acknowledgement.

"Here you go, Mr. Boyd. Would you like anything else, sir?" Marcia said with a smile.

"I'm good for now, Marcia." Choke rubbed the small of her back. She sashayed off to the kitchen.

"I like the old way of things. Honor, loyalty, trust. Doing the job with no questions. The code. Remember?" Clever said as he stood up from the glass table.

"Of course, I remember. We enjoying the fruits of the code." Choke replied, leaning back in the chair, flaunting.

"Yeah... For how long? The Neckman not built like us. The dumb shit he do, and the rules he live by won't last long. And you know it. Before you know it, you'll be robbed like Doug Jones. The first time you get relax -"

"Relax? Who?" Choke jumped to his feet, interrupting Clever.

"You losing focus. Look at you." Clever replied after taking a sip.

"I'm well focus. You look at me. And his name is, The Headless Horseman. Doug Jones... Lost sight of reality with that bullshit he surrounded himself with. Doug Jones weak for pussy. I fuck pussy, and push on. I remember times when I had to save you. Remember?" Choke shot back. He brushed shoulders with Clever on his way to the mini bar.

Choke poured himself a mix of Hennessey and Patron in a crusted clustered Brandolini D'Adda's glass. Watching his partner through the bar's mirror, he downed the concoction cowboy style.

"I was young."

"And? You never thanked me." Choke calmly replied while pouring another concoction.

33

Chapter Six

Choke swirled the concoction around while looking at the time on the Rolex.

"So... What is you saying?" Clever asked, stroking his goatee as he leaned against the patio door. He had placed the empty glass on the window seal, waiting on Choke's reply.

"I know what I'm do -. Yes, Marcia?" Choke paused.

"Would you like dessert, Mr. Boyd," she asked, looking back over her right shoulder, with her hands full of dirty dishes.

Clever waited quietly, in deep thought, watching Marcia's petite frame move around gracefully, handling the dishes.

"Not right now... Cut the back porch light off, and you can resume tomorrow." Choke replied.

"Okay, Mr. Boyd. Good night, sir."

Clever eyed Marcia until she disappeared. He walked over to Choke, staring him in the eyes the whole time. "So, umm... What are you doing?"

"Something that old man Zahager wouldn't allow me to do. You know what, Clever? You ungrateful as fuck." Choke took a step back, looking over Clever's shoulder and seeing The Headless Horseman coming towards them from the kitchen. Clever double blinked in the mirror before turning around quickly unbuttoning the vest he was wearing.

"No need for that... Take a seat. Rest your nerves." The Headless Horseman said. In his right hand was a shiny stainless steel machete. Choke had pulled his gun, and pressed the cold steel barrel against the small of Clever's back.

***

Investigators, medical examiners and forensic crews were scurrying about with notepads, jotting down theories and tapping away with anger. Danielle was sitting in the back of an ambulance while Blot was being interrogated by ten detectives - all dressed in long trench coats with sporty top hats. Standing near the rear side of the coroner van, they showed him no mercy at all.

"Ma'am, do you have any next to kin who will come pick you up," on of the medical examiners asked in the process of taking her vital signs.

Lost in thought, life, self and help, Danielle felt empty inside. The tears started flowing all over again.

"You do know, the only way they can help you is, by you helping them?" The medical examiner said. She readjusted Danielle's arm on her lap and continued working.

Danielle sat in the ambulance, looking for an escape from the horror of the day. All she could think of was her cousin Ice. The ambulance rear door was snatched open, startling both of them. It was a female detective.

"Good luck," the medical examiner said, hopping from the ambulance. Seeing Blot, she turned her nose up.

The neighbors began coming outside of their homes, breaking their code of minding their own business.

"What the hell happened in there," the detective lashed out at Danielle, her face just inches away from hers. Danielle was all sniffles, no words.

"You can stop all that.. One of you knows something. His ass going to jail. You can join his ass, for all I care. So, start talking." The detective said with no emotion while pointing the pen in the direction of her house. Just more sniffles, trembling and tears came from Danielle.

"You need to start talking, before I lock your ass up. It's two men in there dead. In your house."

"I... I... I... Don't know." Danielle managed to stutter.

"You got to be fucking kidding me. Your neighbors told us, you been here all day. Your house full of bullet holes. We found a bag, containing a large quantity of illegal cannabis. Is this a dope house? You know something."

The front doors of the ambulance opened up with two EMTs having a conversation, which caused Danielle to look towards the open partition window.

"Is this yours," the driver asked Danielle, holding up a Natural Cure book and a black pouch so she could see it.

"That's mines," she shouted. She made an attempt to grab it, but was stopped short by the detective's voice.

"Sit down, ma'am. Your night just got longer."

***

"Where are we heading this late," asked Peach.

"Somewhere I don't want to go," Stunna replied. They were headed east on 285 in the express lane.

"Where's that? Because I ain't got time for no nonsense."

"Nah. We going to DeKalb County Jail."

"For what?"

"Gotta bond this shawty out who know how the nigga look who killed Mollie."

Hearing Stunna's response to her question, Peach's tongue was glued to the roof of her mouth like her body was to the seat. He looked over at her, and back to the expressway, knowing she didn't mind the ride.

***

"You gotta hit the schoolhouse tomorrow, Sqizzle."

"I'm gon go, but I ain't staying," Sqizzle replied, looking out the window with a stone cold facial expression.

Mainlife was switching lanes on the expressway, heading west on 285 in a stolen Buick Le Sabre. "Why you not staying?"

"We gotta lay this nigga down before New Years. Safari Malice don fucked up."

Mainlife turned right down Ashby off the expressway on Joseph E. Lowery. "We gon bring the year in right. We got a name on this clown - just need to know how he look."

"It's hot over here. That's the fourth police car I've seen since we jumped off the expressway."

"Shit ain't unusual. Every Westside I been on, be crawling with cops. I got a homie over here. Jo official."

"Who?"

"Hollywood Rell. We on it. If we have to get a little, he with the demonstration."

Mainlife drove through a green light, crossing over Martin Luther King Dr, peeping through the rearview mirror. Sqizzle let the gremlin rest on his lap, surveying the territory they were driving through. They passed a mom and pops food restaurant named Tasty Dogs, eyeing a group standing out front.

"Up there."

Sqizzle looked in the direction Mainlife pointed, and picked up the gun. Music floated through the window as he lowered it. A party was in full effect. He smiled, and Mainlife nodded and stopped the car.

"Where the party at," Mainlife yelled as Sqizzle slid to the backseat.

"Nechelle house," a young boy yelled back, crossing the street with a group of children.

"Aye! Aye! Y'all come here for a minute. Who can tell me where Freddie at?"

"Freddie dead, man!"

"Dead? Where Bugger and Dog?" Mainlife questioned.

38

"Over Nechelle! Who is you?" The little boy walked up to the window as the other children ran off to the store.

"A friend. Watch yourself youngster. Let me get to the party." Mainlife drove off. "I knew his loud mouth ass would get it. Let's check these other niggas out." He turned in to the apartment complex.

"Who is Freddie," asked Sqizzle.

"One of the niggas me and bro had static with on the Malcolm goose chase. This look like Bugger right here." He kept an eye on the man as he drove up next to him, sitting on the hood of a car. "Where the party at?"

"What party," the man responded, blowing out cigarette smoke.

Sqizzle sat slouched in the backseat, eyeing the man and the crowd of people who stood towards the back of the apartments.

"Nechelle."

"Down there," the man pointed. He got off the hood of the car, looking over the parking lot.

Mainlife watched the man closely before pulling off. "That's the nigga, Dog." Sqizzle eased up as he turned around at the dumpsters. On the second floor landing of the apartment people were walking with lit candles in their hands.

"This a memorial party," Sqizzle said.

"Looks that way. They enjoying themselves. Ain't they? Let's give them something to remember." Mainlife said.

Dog stood, looking up in the sky with a 40oz Colt 45, pouring it out.

"Dog?"

"Who the fuck is you?"

"Mainlife!"

Bladadah! Bladadah! Bladadah! Bladadah! Shots rang out loud, and Mainlife stomped on the gas as everybody dropped candles and scrambled for cover.

Boc! Boc! Boc! Boc! The back window of the Buick Le Sabre shattered from the return fire. Mainlife ducked, seeing the group of men in front of Tasty Dog aiming and shooting at him. The steel frame was shielding them like a bulletproof vest.

"We should've hit them niggas up at the Tasty Dog. Fuck niggas tried to get off!" Sqizzle said, looking out the shattered back window as Mainlife turned right on James P. Brawley.

Chapter Seven

The wee hours of the night had come and gone, leaving more problems than solutions. Christmas was fast approaching for the naughty as well as the nice as long as souls continued breathing. As it was another year gone and one on the horizon, the sun rose. But who cared about today?

Crime was on a rise all over the city. Tears of pain, sorrow and anguish had become the norm. Blue skies was being wrestled down by darkness, circumstances continued to cause cigarettes to be chain smoked. Doug Jones and Str 1 sat in front of the 80 inch monitor, watching the surveillance camera inside of the torture dungeon.

"So, you had more niggas? They all gonna die too." Doug Jones said, thrumming the arm of the chair with his fingers.

"Do you... I'm gonna go take care of Leroy sneaky ass. I know he still walking around, trying to get high." Str 1 stood up and grabbed the .45 caliber pistol off the table.

"Nick should've popped his ass for peeping in the windows. Damn, I suppose to let AL hook the sound system to the cameras." Doug Jones said.

"We can't spare shit no more! I be back." Str 1 said before walking out of the room, closing the door behind him.

Doug Jones pressed the zoom in button on the inspector gadget type remote, and slid to the edge of his custom made Dougashi, egg yolk and whip cream colored La -Z Boy. *I must got soft. Niggas just running up in my spots. I'm gon kill y'all, like I offed his ass. I'm still Mr. Untouchable,* he thought to himself. He was boiling with rage as he watched the intruders enter one of his secret hideouts. Watching them lift Safari Malice's limp body put a Joker's smile on his face. He couldn't resist the laughter rising inside.

Doug Jones paused the video footage, making a mental note of all visible tattoos as he stood in front of the screen, pointing the remote at the face of each intruder. Satisfied, with a nod of certainty, he walked across the tiger and lion weaved rug by Alchemy Collection.

***

"Mr. Malone, time to get up. Your breakfast and medicine... Get up and get yourself together. I'll be back to take you to Dr. Zinlish. You're first on the list to get your stitches taken out." Nurse Ashley said, placing the breakfast tray and two pills on the table beside the bed.

Willo, grudgingly, opened his eyes to the brightness of the sun rays flowing through the opened blinders. Wednesday welcomed Willo, but the feeling wasn't mutual for Willo. He looked over at the breakfast tray and sighed, closing his eyes again. Trying to escape reality, he pressed the button that released morphine into the I.V bag, and mellowed out.

Willo took deep breaths slowly, slipping away into the tranquil state the pain reliever brought on. It was all an attempt to forget yesterday. Tahja's funeral got the best of him. Within his heart, he felt the void that stemmed from her absence.

"Mr. Malone! You supposed to be eating. Gone, get up now... Dr. Zinlish not gonna wait on you. Get up and get ready." Nurse Ashley demanded, returning with a contamination bag. She sashayed to another patient's bedside as Willo opened his eyes again with jaws clenched.

Hearing the nurse talking to the other patient, he leaned over and grabbed the toothpaste off the stand. Squeezing a glob of it on the toothbrush, he brushed his teeth while staring at the dust particles that danced about in the sunbeams.

Dr. Yelaski! You're needed in ICU! Dr. Yelaski! The intercom was blasting away in his ears as he spit the toothpaste out in the bowl of grits. *I gotta get the fuck up out of here,* he thought to himself while washing his face. Looking around the room and not paying attention to what he was doing, he brushed the stitches in his chest. "Shit! Not today."

"Ouch! Ouch!" The patient on the other side of the partition screamed.

"Damn, nigga," Willo stressed, not caring to hear it.

***

Marcia made her way through the mini upscale Scarface styled mansion of Choke's to his home office, smiling. "Mr. Boyd, excuse me... There's two gentlemen, by the names of Archibald and Rudy, at the door."

"Show them to the guest room, and give them some drinks. I'll be there in a minute." Choke replied, looking up from the laptop.

Marcia nodded and walked off, heels clanking on the cherry red oak wood floor.

Midday Wednesday

Chapter Eight

As expected, Choke computed figures of the latest shipments, and save it. Archibald and Rudy was right on time. He squeezed the top of his nose, blinking his eyes, regrouping his thoughts before standing. He looked over at the custom made glass aquarium that held an 11 foot albino python after hearing the squeal of the piglet he'd been anticipating. "That's right, Menace... Kill em."

Walking over to the wall length plexiglass tank, he smiled as Menace coiled around his prey. Placing a hand on the tank, he nodded his approval of the red and green eyed predator as it crushed every bone, suffocating the piglet.

***

Blot stood, looking out the blinders in the front room of his house while trying to make sense of yesterday's events.

"So, what now," Danielle asked.

"Go get some rest. Me and Juice gon take care of it. Go upstairs to my room. I promise, we gon handle it." Blot replied, looking at Danielle's figure balled up on the couch in fetal position, eyes red and puffy from crying.

"They killed my cousin," she whispered.

"Come on... You gotta get some sleep. We gon find out who did it."

"They killed him," she slurred out as her eyes rolled to the back of her head.

"Juice," Blot yelled in the process of lifting her body off the couch. He carried her up the stairs. She drooled like an infant on the sleeve of his black Carhort jacket.

"What's up," Juice asked, coming from the kitchen. He waited at the bottom of the stairs seeing the front room was unoccupied. He leaned against the banister and finished the half pint of E and J he had been working on.

"Come on. She out." Blot said, trotting back down the stairs. "Did Hot or Man answer their phones?"

"Bout time she crashed. Them pills supposed to been kicked in." Juice said, emptying the bottle of the last drop.

"You hear me? Did Hot or Man pick up?"

"Hell nah. Them niggas don't be saying shit anyway. This gotta be Ox."

"That beef squashed with Jamaica. Jamaica Ox whole operation shut down. Ice laid the law down on him and his squad. Ox thought it was safe, until we got his vault. The nigga went missing after that. Where the fuck is Hot and Man?"

"Fuck them niggas. They some new niggas anyway. What we bout to do?" Juice said.

"I don't know. I gotta check in with Loco for show. Let him know what happened... Huh, here go fifty. Make sure she don't go nowhere."

"Blot, I ain't doing no babysitting."

"Get off that shit, Juice. If it wasn't for her, yo ass wouldn't be here."

"What you mean by that," asked Juice.

"You still breathing, nigga. Fuck you mean?" Blot shot back.

Juice took a step back, looking at Blot sideways. Blot stared back into his eyes, before picking up the half eaten hot pocket and heading for the front door.

"Get that nigga name," Blot said demandingly as he left.

Juice remained standing, gritting his teeth, remembering when Ice had took him to Danielle after being stabbed in the chest by a female at Club Crucial. The incident had been the hottest topic up and down Bankhead Highway for months last year. He still thirsted for revenge on the woman who told him she was a man handler.

***

Choke turned the light off in the office seeing Menace wasn't hungry - as he'd expected. Menace killed the piglet, and uncoiled, stretching out to fill the length of the aquarium. "Marcia, you can leave now."

"Okay, sir," she replied and walked off, leaving then speechless in their lustful state.

"Y'all enjoying yourselves," Choke asked, looking at the desire written all over the faces of his Panamanian companions who sat sipping top dollar wine comfortably.

"Nah... Where the best of drink? You getting like Jack, watering down the drinks at your house." The muscle of the two said as he drained the glass of its content, shaking his head.

"Rudy, that's topnotch. Louie Thirteenth. Archibald ain't complaining."

"Aye... This the only time I relax. House business. You got everything situated?" Archibald said, lifting the briefcase that sat next to his chair.

"Since when you know me not to be ready?"

Archibald and Choke stared each other down with knowing intentions as Rudy popped his knuckles.

"We checked out the areas around Simpson Rd and the Bluff. It's good traffic. But, if this going to work, we going to need you to handle this."

"Handle what?"

Archibald opened the briefcase, grabbed a manilla envelope, and slid it across the table. Rudy looked on, stroking his goatee. Choke ripped the envelope open and dumped the contents out on the table. A couple of pictures landed, facing up, causing him to grunt loudly.

"What gives," asked Choke, sliding the pictures to the side.

"Business," Rudy replied as he and Archibald looked at each other with raised eyebrows.

"Loyalty is everything. You do know that?" Archibald stated while sliding another envelope across the table. Hesitant and confused, Choke opened it and shook its contents out ad well. A single photo leafed its way to the table, and landed face down.

"Trust me... Y'all wouldn't be in my house if I had any issues with loyalty." Choke said, turning the picture over.

"You know the game getting younger, and it's changing. It's not the 80's, like when you started hustling." Archibald said while tapping the glass table with his right index finger.

"Do you know them," asked Rudy after clearing his throat.

"I don't know her," Choke replied, sliding the photo towards Rudy.

"Her name is, T-la. What about them?" Archibald asked, pointing at the first two pictures.

"What's their names," asked Rudy. Seeing Choke stand caused him to do the same.

"This Keith. The Politician. He stay over there by the governor mansion." He answered, before looking at the other picture.

"It's good you know where he stay. No direction needed."

"And he work for me. What kind of job is this?"

"Favor for a favor," Rudy replied while they walked to the mini bar.

"Favor for a favor? I don't mind them two, but he's one of mines. Any dirty business for them, no problem. But him... I can't do it."

"Well... What's his name?" Archibald asked.

"No need for it. He one of mines. Now, if you want me to handle them, cool. If not... We done. I can deal with him."

"Take care of The Politician. Just be aware of her." Rudy said. The two Panamanians nodded, and showed themselves out.

Choke watched them leave from the dining room window. Returning to the table, he picked up the picture of T-la, and studied it some more, before picking up the Headless Horseman's picture.

***

Detective Thomas was patrolling with a picture of an alledged suspect Kroger's Plaza on Moreland Avenue, seeking information on the murders and shootings several weeks prior on Confederate Avenue. "Have you seen this man," he asked a group of people coming out of Pizza Hut as he held up the 8.5 x 11 in photocopy photo. Cold stares and middle fingers was the answer he received.

Detective Thomas walked off and sat on the hood of the unmarked Crown Victoria. Tapping the photo against his right knee, he surveyed the commercial businesses that made up the plaza. Moreland Avenue was cluttered with holiday commuters and Christmas shoppers, enjoying the day. He radioed in for assistance. Being it was his first year as detective and first major case, he was determined to prove himself an asset to his department.

"Excuse me, sir... Have you seen this man?"

"Who it is, Daddy," the little girl asked her father, who held her in his arms. The man stared at Detective Thomas.

Atlanta

Chapter Nine

The man didn't blink as he stared at the detective. "I'm not looking for him." He popped his daughter on the hand for reaching at the photo.

"This man is dangerous and wanted."

"So am I," the man replied before walking off, whispering in his daughter's left ear as she nodded her head up and down.

Detective Thomas looked on with a sour face as the little girl started laughing. After watching the little girl being tickled by her father, he walked back to his car, and waited for assistance.

***

Juice opened the door to a back room, and laid eyes on Safari Malice. Flaring his nose, he rushed to the corner he was laying in. "Get yo ass up!"

Safari Malice's eyes fluttered open halfway as he grunted and cringed in pain.

"The hell with that... Do it hurt? What's yo name?" Juice wanted answers. He pressed Safari against the wall, bearing his 5'11 and 225 pounds frame on him. "Open your mouth nigga! Ice dead because of you! He should've let me snuff yo ass! Open yo mouth!"

The pain he was feeling overpowered his ability to respond.

"What's yo name," Juice asked in the midst of delivering blows to his body.

"Safari," he managed to reply.

"Safari what? Open yo mouth, nigga!" Juice punched him in the face.

"Juice! Stop!"

He turned around after hearing Danielle's voice. The hate in his eyes and expression was indefinable. "Get out of here! Go back to sleep."

"Why you doing that," she questioned.

"Do you know his name," he yelled with a stern look on his face. Safari Malice's body twitched violently. Danielle just stared. "I didn't think so. Now, get out of the way. What's yo name?"

Juice threw a couple solid blows to Safari Malice's stomach, causing him to cough up blood.

"Stop it!"

"What? What you need to do is, take your ass back upstairs and go to sleep." Juice demanded.

"You going to kill him," Danielle screamed as she broke down in tears.

"Get out my way," Juice said as he stood up and pushed passed her with blood dripping from his hands.

***

"What you doing for Christmas Break, Sqizzle?"

"Shit... I don't know, Dimp. I'm bout to bounce though."

The school's cafeteria was packed with students and teachers as Sqizzle and Dimp sat, talking.

"Me and Brann gon have Capitol Homes jumping. Pull up."

"I'll try, bro. I'm still trying to find the nigga who killed my uncle."

"Say no more. Get at us if you need us."

"Alright. I'm gon swing through with bro and them for show on New Years."

"Cap or die. Stay up, homie. I'm bout to catch this dice game on the roof. Win some of that free money from them Trestle Tree niggas."

"Cool. I'm out." Sqizzle maneuvered through the crowd, heading for the exit as Dimp hurried to the roof of South Side Highschool.

***

"When y'all gon let me go, or move dude," Willo asked the nurse as she wheeled him around the hospital in the wheelchair to Dr. Zinlish's office.

"That's not up to me," she responded.

"Ouch! What's wrong with you?" Willo complained, rubbing his neck as they were bypassing a gift shop. She'd swerved the wheelchair into the wall intentionally.

"Why you spit in those grits? I know your mama taught you better than that. If you didn't want to eat it, you should've left it as is. That was disgusting."

"Well, y'all need to fire whoever cooked that shit."

"Watch your mouth."

"Ah... Man."

"I'm a woman. Get it right."

"Hell, I gotta watch my neck... And hell isn't a bad word either." Willo said.

"Child..."

"See, that's why I get along with High-Top. He understands me." Willo complained.

"Do you understand him," Nurse Ashley asked, knowing the answer.

***

Blot sat, furious, as he parked in front of a vacant lot on Dill Avenue. He eyed the traffic in his brown Tahoe as he waited on Loco to come out of Auto Zone. *Where the fuck these lil niggas at? I know they see my number... I'm done fucking with these niggas after this. Damn, Ice. How the fuck you and Dig get caught slipping?* He thought to himself.

With the music volume on low, he tried to make the best of the situation, replaying the last moves Ice set up. Sorting the assumptions out like a game of Tetris, Blot didn't notice the police car make a u-turn behind him.

Thud! Thud! The knocks on the window got his attention to the fullness.

"Open up!"

Blot looked into the man's face, and knew he was mad. "I don't know what happened, Loco."

"Yeah? Alright. Spin over to College Park." Loco replied nonchalantly.

***

Nurse Ashley smiled and greeted people as she wheeled Willo to the doctor's office. "Listen, young man. I know you're not disrespectful around Mr. James because I know he don't put up with foolishness. So, you're not going to act ignorant around me either."

"Cool. I can adjust if it means you'll stop hitting me like I'm your child."

"When you're under my care, you is," she replied with a smile as the doctor's office came into view.

"I thought you said Dr. Zanleach would be ready," Willo said, seeing all the patients who seemed to be waiting to see the doctor.

"It's pronounced Zin-lish."

"Zenlesh... He need to hurry up."

"Dr. Zinlish is a lady. And never rush a woman or your doctor. Neither ends well. Would you like to read a magazine while waiting?"

"Nah, I'm straight. She need to tighten up and get this over with, before I take em out myself."

"Child, you better learn patience. Wait here while I go sign you in."

Willo had a dull look on his face as the nurse walked off. The sound of a baby crying averted his attention to the entrance of the waiting room. A black woman, who he could tell was exhausted, in a bedroom robe and boots, came walking in with her baby wrapped in layers of blankets.

***

Mainlife started the day off downing a personal bottle of Hennessey as he pulled up on Stunna on Hill Street.

Chapter Ten

"To you, Mollie. Long live Mollie." Mainlife said as he poured out the rest of the Hennessey on the curb before slinging the bottle. The shattering bottle stopped an elderly woman in her tracks as she looked around at the number 4 bus stop, while the bus pulled up.

Mainlife made it up the front porch and waited as Stunna unlocked the door.

"What it do, fam," Stunna asked opening the door.

"Much love, bro."

"United we be."

"United we stand. You know you owe us 200 a piece for not answering your phone. Where you go?"

"I told you, I had to check on something," Stunna replied while locking the door again.

"What the fuck happened to you," Mainlife yelled, seeing T-la on the couch.

"Calm down, fool... I was in an accident." She said. Her left arm was in a makeshift sling. She was propped up on her right side, smoking a blunt.

"Damn... What the fuck you was doing?" Mainlife said as T-la passed him the blunt.

"Playing Rambo," Stunna butted in, taking a seat.

"Whatever, Stunna... I was checking some lames in Sandy Springs. They put the police on me awhile back." T-la said.

"Right. Right. I need to take you to Chicago. You be wilding. My crazy ass sisters will fuck with you off the dribble." Mainlife replied.

"I was raised like this... Tay and Fly didn't play. Somebody walking to the backdoor." T-la said.

Seeing the shadow pass the window, Stunna got up and met the fiend who was trying to pacify his craving for the morning.

"You know them M.G.M.D shorties will fuck with your game. Tip and Black Girl get it in too. You stay in some shit." Mainlife said as he turned on the television and relaxed on the couch.

"Yeah, I heard about them, but I'm Gucci. They got their own shit going on, and I got mines. You know how I function." T-la replied.

"For show. I know Tip and Black Girl personally. They one hundred. Y'all should link up, flush the streets. I know you got your Man Handling shit going on. Where you can't go, they can... Like your Sandy Springs problem."

T-la stared at Mainlife in deep thought as the news went to commercial break. "I heard y'all crashed the funeral."

"Crashed hell. Matter fact. What's up with this Safari Malice?"

"He's a Jack boy. He robbed Doug Jones. Doug put a price tag on his head." T-la replied.

"I'm cashing his ass in. He the vic who lit Willo up."

"How you know that," asked T-la.

"Shit... Me and Sqizzle was doing some dot to dot shit. Shorty came in the funeral with a smoke pole'blazing, screaming Safari killed Taj while aiming at Willo's chest."

T-la's mouth was opened wide as she leaned forward, adjusting the sling. "I got something for his ass. Stunna know?"

"You gee," asked Mainlife.

"Yeah," T-la responded through gritting teeth.

"Yo shit broke?"

"Nah. I was leaning on it too hard. I'm straight..."

"Stunna know want," Stunna came in asking after hearing his name.

***

Detective Thomas and Officer David stood in the Kroger's Plaza overlooking the parking lot, sipping coffee as people were overlooking them.

"They don't care about us, so you don't care about them. We're policemen. I know they hate me, because I make them hate me. You have to get the job done.

"The other day, I was called to investigate a shooting incident... Check this. When I get to the area... Nobody knows anything.

"What kind of shit is that? Here I am, trying to serve and protect them. Fucking assholes. See, Thomas, you got to be the detective - get more aggressive out here. Don't accept no for an answer." Officer David said, lighting a cigarette.

"I understand," Detective Thomas replied.

"Do you," asked Officer David.

"Yeah. But why you not a detective?"

"Detective? Thomas, who say I'm not? I told you, you have to be the detective. This officer shit is just a throw off. If I have to do a fucking job, I do it. Justice starts with us. Let the courts sort the shit out. I lock em up, and let the DA throw away the key."

Officer David and Detective Thomas were day and night. Opposites, but committed to the same force and creed.

"Detective Thomas, they'll kill you in a heartbeat out here. Don't be a fool." Officer David was dressed in his uniform he had custom designed from years on the force - a T-shirt with slacks.

Detective Thomas scanned the parking lot, scratching his head, looking like Carl Winslow as Officer David, looking like Popeye, posted, looking from franchise to franchise.

***

"Cocoa butter will smooth that out," the nurse said, watching Willo touch the scar the stitches left.

"How you know?"

"My job and first child," Nurse Ashley replied. She stopped the wheelchair at the elevator and wiped her forehead. The elevator doors opened a second later. A crowd poured out of the space, carrying on conversations, bumping into them without saying excuse me.

"Hey! Watch the fuck out!" Willo yelled, trying to protect his leg.

"I have a patient here. Excuse us." The nurse said respectfully, which caused the crowd to stop and move aside. "I thank you kindly. Enjoy the rest of your day." She wheeled Willo into the elevator, and with a jerk, it begun ascending.

"It stinks in here," Willo complained.

"That it does. It's getting close to my break."

"It's time for me to break out of here. I didn't know you had that in you. They thought they was just gonna run us over."

"Don't think I didn't hear you... I'm not going to hit you. Relax. It was needed at that moment." Nurse Ashley said as Willo lifted his head.

"I'm just saying... They deserved it. Look at me... I'm down bad."

"You can't act ugly just because the next person is being ugly."

"You sounding like Mr. James with all that philosophy."

Thank you for the complement. You right, because I listen when he talk. He's a real man of God. How far do you think you'll make it with your attitude?"

"I'm no pushover."

"It's not about being a pushover. It's about using your brain. You gotta start thinking."

"I do use my brain," Willo said defensively.

The elevator came to a stop, and the nurse gripped the arms of the wheelchair. "Excuse us. We're getting off."

"Pull around back and park," Loco demanded.

Hostile

Chapter Eleven

Blot felt the tension grow as Loco stared at him, listening. The secluded area was ran down. They were parked behind a redbrick building with wood pallets and milk crates stacked everywhere.

"It's crazy. For real." Blot said after explaining.

"Nah... It ain't crazy. You listen to me. I want my money or work. Death don't stop my money, especially not another nigga.

"You, Juice and them new niggas, better come up with something. Blot, you know this game is deadly." Loco replied, shifting his gaze to the sky blue Camaro SS pulling up.

"We ain't got no money, and the work was taken with the weed. I'm telling you face to face what happened, Loco."

"OK... You told me, and I told you." Loco said before getting out of the Tahoe. He walked over to the Camaro without looking back.

Blot was left, looking dumbfounded. He watched Loco movements. Loco opened the trunk and the driver got out the car. He stood mugging him.

Dadah! Dadah! Dadah! Loco lowered the smoking Tech-9 and slammed the trunk.

Blot put the Tahoe in reverse, backing out as Loco walked to the passenger's side of the Camaro with gun swaying in his right hand.

"Bloomfield," the driver yelled, throwing up his hands, watching Blot swerve, crashing into pallets and crates while fleeing the scene.

***

Choke pulled into his driveway, keeping his eyes on the surrounding. After riding by Keith the Politician residence on Paces Ferry Road, he wanted nothing more than to get the job done. Random thoughts about the Headless Horseman entered his mind, creating the image of him posing at one of his long archenemy's gambling houses.

"You did what?"

"You heard me. I filed for divorce. It's over!"

"Nah... Nah... You got me. I'm not going nowhere for another bitch to come up in here. Nigga, you crazy!"

Marcia turned around quickly from watching the BET movie upon hearing Choke entering the house, talking on his phone. His crocodile wildlife box tips were sounding off on the hardwood floor as he walked by the couch. She stood to greet him, but seeing the look in his eyes, she reluctantly returned to her quarters within the mansion.

Making it to the office, Choke slammed the door behind him, sending pictures crashing to the floor. The echo caused Marcia to flinch. Frightened, she began speaking rapidly in her native tongue.

"Now, listen. I need you on standby tonight. I gotta kill 2 birds with 1 stone... Mr. Porter not going to do business without Clever." Choke spoke into the receiver as he paced the floor.

"So, what do you want me to do," asked the Headless Horseman.

"Clean him up. I'm gon make sure he don't try nothing." Choke ended the call and focused his attention on Menace slithering and flickering his tongue inside the aquarium. "Did you hear me?" He walked off from the tank.

"I'm done," the Headless Horseman called back and replied between winded breaths, which got raised eyebrows from Choke.

"You done? What the hell that mean?"

"I finished what he wanted me to do."

"Bring him tonight!" Choke demanded. He knew how much he hated Clever. Ending the call, he left the office, crushing the broken frames under the weight of his feet.

Choke strolled through the mansion, paying little attention to the accumulated wealth. Flashes of Clever voicing his opinion about the Headless Horseman danced in his mind. Was the Headless Horseman still reliable, he wondered as he walked out on the balcony.

***

The Headless Horseman sat looking at Clever's severed head and his gouged out eyes that floated in chemicals inside of a preservative jar. Admiring a job well done, he paid Choke's words no mind.

"Somebody wanted to see you... You can get a headstart or I can take a piece of you. Your choice. Choose wisely, and be quick about it." The Headless Horseman said, staring at Clever's head.

He stood up and stepped over it while rummaging through his pockets. Pulling out a clear baggie with white substance, he emptied the content on the bloody machete and tooted it up his nose. "What's your choice?"

Clever's body parts were sprawled out like an undone jigsaw puzzle. The Headless Horseman had dismembered him and placed every organ into jars he sealed lids with Gorilla Glue. He smiled with blood mixed with coke on the tip of his nose as sweat beaded on his bald head.

Stirring bleach and ammonia in a mop bucket, he envisioned his new duck off spot at Clever's expense. The luxury house in East Point off Sylvan Road and Milledge Street was perfect for the taking.

***

Blot cursed his way to the red light, riding without any music playing. How had it come to this, he wondered. He looked over at a black Ford F-150 on 30 inch gold rims. The woman, riding by herself swayed to the sound of the music, smiled and waved at him.

The lady flushed off, gassing the truck under the green light with Blot switching lanes behind her. He threw the cellphone onto the passenger's seat. Tailing her down Main Street, he bit on his bottom lip while he kept an eye out for the sign of police as he gunned through intersections.

"Get the fuck out the way," he screamed while honking the horn at the T-Top Thunderbird that cut him off. The two old school players who occupied the car were absorbed in the O'Jays to pay him any mind. "Stupid muthafuckas!" He accelerated around them and spit out the window.

Traffic was cluttering as he tried to catch up to the F-150 without trying to be noticed. He picked up the phone, and called Juice. He cut three cars off on a right away as they tried to turn in Winn Dixie's

Supermarket parking lot. He closed the gap between him and the F-150 to four car lengths.

"Damn... Nigga! Answer the fucking phone!" He screamed, leaving Juice a voicemail before dialing the number again.

***

Detective Thomas trailed Officer David through the neighboring community around Kroger's Plaza. Asking questions and demanding answers, Detective Thomas wasn't taking no for an answer - thanks to the pep talk he'd received from Officer David. The unmarked Crown Victoria and police cruiser, brought crazy looks and fast footwork as they were bumper to bumper driving.

Detective Thomas wanted the suspect responsible for the senseless shootings on Confederate Avenue. A couple victims were left wounded in critical condition, and two were dead, according to the reports. His heart wouldn't allow him to give up and put the case aside - in the cold case files. Writing off such malicious intent wasn't something he was willing to come to terms with

Looking at the case file on the passenger's seat, Detective Thomas vowed to solve the case.

***

Stunna was weighing Ebony's actions in his mind while sitting at a red light with Mainlife and T-la small talking. In his mind, he knew his Uncle Mollie's killer would soon meet his fate. Safari Malice, your ass belongs to me, he thought to himself, smiling because of the new information he'd received from Ebony.

It is... What it is

Chapter Twelve

"Bro, we gotta lay this nigga down before New Year. We owe Mollie and Lil Moll Moll, man. So, where Ebony? She know how he look."

Stunna slowed down behind the Marta bus as it cruised at 3 miles per hour after picking up passengers.

"She over Peach house. T-la, where you going after this?"

"I'm riding with y'all. I wanna get at that nigga too."

"Nah.. You need to go get some rest." Stunna protested as he pressed pause on the CD player, muting the Yung Marley S.G.E Mixtape. He eyed Chef B's Soul Food restaurant and turned on the left blinker, sliding into the turning lane.

"I'm good. I'm not gonna let this shit slow me down. My Uncle Tay and Fly raised a gangsta." T-la said to her defense.

"You always on that," Stunna said with laughter.

Boulevard traffic was mild. As a few drivers made U- turns, Stunna pulled in the parking lot of Chef Band and observed the traffic.

"I told her, she need to come to the Go," Mainlife said.

Stunna shook his head. "She ain't ready for that gang land. Chicago too much for her." Stunna replied.

"Mainlife ain't in no gang," T-la shot back while adjusting the sling as she got out the car.

"It's in my blood," Mainlife said.

"G.T.C is too! Grant Top Committee!" Stunna yelled, opening the restaurant door.

Mainlife and Stunna laughed, entering the crowded establishment. T-la, on the other hand, pushed pass them, shaking her head and looking for an empty booth. Jazz played softly and the aroma of well seasoned food filled the air. The place was lively; the sound of laughter, silver wear clanking against China wear - the holiday spirit was in full affect at Chef B's.

"It's a booth over there," T-la said, leading the way and flagging down a black rock star looking male waiter.

"Order the fried hot wings smothered in hot sauce for me. I'll be back." Mainlife said.

"Where the hell you going," Stunna asked as he walked off. Mainlife was middle ways across the restaurant before Stunna could finish the question.

T-la eased in a booth as the waiter placed menus on the table. A baritone voice came across the loudspeaker, announcing the next musical piece by Kenny Garret called A Silent Prayer.

The lady was taken by surprise after being tapped on the shoulder by Mainlife as she was talking with a group. Turning around, she eyed him closely, seeing his red half closed eyes and a smirk on his face.

"Boy, don't be sneaking up on me," she said teasingly as her friends looked on quizzically.

"You always somewhere running your mouth. Carrie, what's up with you?" Mainlife replied, guiding her out of earshot of her friends.

Stunna peeped Mainlife's destination and the group of women around him before catching up with T-la, who sat sipping on a glass of Cognac.

"Slow down. What you order?" Stunna said.

"Nothing yet. I gotta get my drink on." T-la replied.

Stunna watched T-la rotate her injured shoulder, acknowledging the fact that she was a true soldier.

"Are you ready to order, ma'am," the waiter asked, looking T-la over through the coke bottle frame bifocals. His accent was one of the deep south.

"Yeah. I'll have oxtails and the Auntie Jean Vegetable Bowl with Jalapeño Bread." T-la replied.

"And you, sir," the waiter turned to Stunna asking.

"You can't be from the city... Give me the barbeque steak strips plate and the Uncle Bo's Macaroni Special and Grandpa Noah's Fried Hot Wings smothered in hot sauce and the Seasoned Grandma Naomi's Collard Greens." Stunna said.

"Coming right up," he replied as he walked off, scribbling on the flip pad.

"Let me slide in with you, T-la," Mainlife said, returning to the table. "Stunna, we locked in now."

"Who shawty was," Stunna asked, placing his phone back in his pocket.

"West Coast's cousin, Carrie."

Stunna's eyebrows were raised as he leaned back and was all ears.

"Where," T-la inquired, turning around.

"You know West Coast," Mainlife asked T-la as she tried her best to spot Carrie.

"Yeah... Enough that he's on my man handling list. Where she at?"

***

Sqizzle's agenda changed for the day after receiving a call from York. Parked at the South Gate of the Greyhound Station, he smoked a Newport, watching as families and friends greeted their love ones and York unload the bus.

***

"Ebo! You seen the keys? Willo getting out!" N. O yelled while tossing cushions off the couch, searching for the car keys.

***

I'm ready, sun. You know New York niggas pop off? Where your peeps?" York said, rolling a Backwood cigar full of Sour Diesel, a potent grade of marijuana.

"They riding. I want to catch the nigga before them."

"All you got is his name.. Safari Malice?"

"Yeah. Mainlife took me over to the nigga location last night. But the nigga been moved. They getting more info on him now." Sqizzle said as they waited at Checkers on Cleveland Avenue for their food.

Sqizzle and York sat, watching the movements of a known drug infested area that Sqizzle wanted. The operation was like clock work, which was the reason he had his sights on it in the first place. The only missing piece was, the whereabouts of its unknown leader, who wasn't known by workers or customers. He'd received a name from a stripper who worked at Dream Girl, six weeks ago - Phantom.

Not knowing the identity of Phantom, Sqizzle stall pursued.

"Look," York said, grabbing the Checkers' carryout bag while exhaling weed smoke.

They observed the school bus heading down Cleveland Avenue in reverse, causing traffic to clutter.

"Shit like that will make a nigga smoke. Welcome to the real dirty south. Shit ain't happening like this in New York." Sqizzle said.

"Yo, sun, we got hella shit popping. Oh shit! This nigga bugging!" York said, passing Sqizzle the blunt.

***

"Hell yeah! It was a shootout at the video shoot off Campbelton Road. Dirty Life street as fuck. Mix him with that booty shaking shit if you wanna. He did that for the hoes." E-bo said, tossing the keys to N.O after finding then inside of the weed jar in his room.

"E-bo, you tripping. I'm not messing with dude. Boss Fam Lady A slapped him in the face bout her studio time when the nigga was a engineer, mixing niggas shit. I been got the ups on dude.

"He ain't popping like S.G.E's Yung Marley, SQ Tha Bare Face Robber, Crazy Crazy, Boss Life Bigg. Not to mention, D-Stack Hope, Demon Child..."

"Damn nigga, you gon name everybody? I get the point." E-bo said, cutting N.O off. He slammed the passenger's side door of the red box Chevy.

"Play this. It's a new track. He got the nigga Bigg Main on the hook." N.O said.

"Yeah, alright. If it's some bullshit, I'm slinging it out the window." E-bo replied.

Chapter Thirteen

N.O was unaware of his bobbing as E-bo split a Swisher Sweet down the middle, looking at him smiling. "What's his name again?"

"Bigg Main. He got 2pac in him." N.O said as the first verse ended, and Dirty Life sounded throughout the car.

"I'm out the streets. Repping East..."

"No, you not," N.O said, hitting pause on the CD player.

"Damn, nigga. You ain't let the nigga ride." E-bo said as they pulled up behind a motorcycle at a stop sign.

"I know. I never brushed passed him out here or in the club. You ready to puff, puff, pass?" N.O replied as E-bo put fire to the blunt.

"Get off that. You be listening to niggas that's not from the city."

"Yeah, cause they ain't on no studio gangsta shit unlike the niggas in the city. Solid niggas get murked by fucking with flaw ass niggas like him."

***

The day had its dilemma as time ticked down. The afternoon sunshine faded from high noon towards the evening sky. Sqizzle and York was caught in the moment, staring at an accident the school bus caused as a teen raced pass them with another one at a distance, yelling as he slow dragged, looking at the accident.

"Hot, get me two of them Chili Checkers Burgers! I'm bout to watch this!"

"Man, you bullshitting. Fuck that accident. You see that shit everyday. Hurry up, before you get left." Hot replied as the Checkers' manager walked pass him on the phone.

"Look at that shit... We pushing that 88 pure. Them smokers bout to be rushing us."

"You know Rack feeling himself."

"Fuck that nigga. He gon be alright."

Sqizzle and York walked back to the car, almost bumping into the Checkers' manager as she was screaming in the phone and pointing wildly. Traffic was at a standstill both ways as the sound of ambulances and police sirens filled the air.

"You heard them loud mouth ass lil niggas," asked York while getting in on the passenger's side.

"Yeah. The nigga, Rack I heard of. He from over here." Sqizzle replied.

"What he on?"

"Nothing too much. He might be working a duce and a pound."

"2 ounces of dope and a pound of what?"

"Mid."

"Okay."

"The nigga is no factor," Sqizzle said as he pulled out of Checkers parking lot. York kept his eyes on Hot and Man as they walked and ate.

"They going to the same apartments... They might know who the Phantom is. Check me in over at the American Inn. Go handle your biz with yo moms." York said, looking at the layout of the hotel's parking lot.

****

Str 1 made it his top priority to find Leroy before he met up with one of the power hitters in the music business. From sponsoring Dirty Life and other buzzing artists, he strived to build an empire out of his music label and dreams. Having his ears to the streets and currency, he received the info on Leroy's whereabouts, and crashed the party.

"Leroy, I know you in there."

Everybody in the dim lit basement froze stiff as the clouds of smoke dazzled about before their eyes. Fear toppled with paranoia kicked in seeing Str 1 holding the SKS assault rifle in his hands. The happy gathering had become a scared straight program.

"Wha, wha, what chu want? No Leroy in here." A female stuttered as she was squeezing between four people behind a couch.

"Leroy ain't in here, bruh," a half-naked man who stood shaking in front of two women by a loveseat.

"I hate being lied to and played. I paid a hundred to be pointed to this location. Now, if you don't know nothing, please shut the fuck up! Who's Diana then? Which one of you broads is Diana?" Str 1 slid the bolt back, putting one in the chamber to reassure them he wasn't playing.

"She gone," a man walked down the stairs and said with three men behind him. He flipped the lights on, revealing the crooked smile on his and two of the three men faces. Str 1 spun around and made eye contact with them. The smokers huddled even closer in their spaces for safety.

"I ain't going out like this," the man in front of the loveseat yelled before putting the crack pipe to his lips and striking the lighter.

"Put that shit out while I'm down here," the leader of the four yelled while stepping on level ground. He exhaled like a freight train, two stepping out the way as Str 1 raised the SKS assault rifle chest level to the group.

"Nah, nigga," Str 1 said, peeping the reaction of the man left of their leader.

"Please! No! Please!" The women cried. They were trying to avoid being shot in the crossfire. From three dollar hits and wanting to party, final destination started looking inescapable for them as Str 1's Houston, Texas blood boiled inside. Without warning, he let loose.

Raqa! Raqa! Raqa!

"Damn! Vice... You got this nigga shit all on a nigga." The lead man said, looking himself over as the other two men scrambled to their feet. The penalty for not knowing Str 1's mentality.

"Dust, you know how I rock."

"Ouch! Ouch!"

Raqa! "Shut the fuck up," Str 1 yelled after letting another round off, hitting Leroy in the head.

The screams became mournful cries and sobs as they looked upon Leroy's lifeless body slumped in a pool of his own blood.

"You gon send somebody to clean this shit up," Dust asked. The other two guys stood speechless.

"I got you. Don't let nobody out. I got a ounce in the car. Cook it and give it to them."

"Damn, bro. You could've warned us." One of the men said while stepping over Leroy's body.

"The nigga didn't care bout Nick, so fuck him. One of y'all come get the dope." Str1 said, brushing pass them. He left a memory in the basement that will never be forgotten.

"You only got your word. If what you say don't hold weight, you're not a man. In these streets, that's all we got. What's your name?" Str 1 said, lifting the purple gym bag from the backseat."

"Webster."

"OK. Take this. Tell Dust it's a duce. This here for you and your peeps. What's his name?"

"Alex," Webster replied, placing the ziploc bag of cocaine and money in his pocket as Str 1 got behind the wheel.

"Web, it's rules in these streets. Here, take these jackets. It's the newest Silent Apparel by the top gunna from Summer Hill, Bully Red. Solid niggas move in silence. Don't forget." Str 1 said, starting the car and taking his phone out of his pocket.

Webster walked off with some extra pep in his step and a smile. His loyalty resided with Dust; however, he felt a growing connection from Str 1's words of wisdom.

***

"Juice! You need to pick up the phone. Loco wants his money. Call me back." Blot ended the voicemail and stared at Juice's number until it faded off the screen. Mobile and angry, he drove the Tahoe through rush hour traffic back to his apartment.

***

The night brought on pursuit at deadly risks. Str 1 navigated the streets with watchful eyes. At twenty six years old and established because of his bond with Doug Jones and upbringing of power, he was solidified in the game, making money moves. Without calling Doug Jones's number, he swerved over to his place of business unannounced, knowing Nick would be glad to see Leroy.

***

Knowing Ms. Mary, Willo knew his answer better have been well thought of before blurting anything out. But, the way he was feeling, he didn't care. As he waited to be picked up, time seemed to move at a snail's pace.

Truth

Chapter Fourteen

"Ms. Mary, I did... I tried talking to her family. They didn't want nothing to do with me. I'm not a bad person... Look at me - I'm the one been shot up." Willo protested.

"I'm sorry to hear that. But, don't give up, son. The wound is still fresh, but it'll heal. If you care about her like you say... Follow through on your word.

"We all make mistakes, child. Not saying, this was your mistake. Her family have to get to know you, so you can show them you're not a bad person." Ms. Mary replied.

"I don't know," he responded, shaking his head.

"You don't have a choice if you still wondering about the baby," she stated and walked out the room singing Amazing Grace. Her choice of words pierced Willo's soul. Willo's nostrils flared up with total madness as he watched the door close.

Dinner was served hot, but he discarded it with resentment, flipping the tray off the stand. Mr. Smith's open partition wasn't a nuisance anymore due to him being relocated to Georgia Regional Mental Institution for biting a nurse's finger off. Alone and lost for thought, Willo was far gone without the snooze button propped up in a wheelchair.

"Snap out of it... Who going to clean this up?" Mr. James said after stepping halfway in the room with Nurse Ashley and Jalise behind him.

"We not," Nurse Ashley replied while walking over to the open partition with fresh linen in her arms.

"I know I'm not. Grady don't pay me that much." Nurse Jalise added as she sat down with a plastic bag in her hand.

Willo shook his head and looked over to Mr. James as he removed the I.V bag. "I need to see the baby."

Mr. James's facial expression was one of concern as he compressed the cords and bag into a clear plastic pouch. "I don't know how you're going to make that happen, other than through prayer. You been praying like I asked you too?"

"If you haven't, now is a better time than any to start," Nurse Jalise chided in, seeing Willo was hesitant.

"Answer the question, boy," Nurse Ashley commanded as she stepped back into the conversation from changing the linen on the other bed.

Everybody's attention turned towards the door as they heard knocks.

"Come in," Mr. James said after Nurse Ashley opened the blinders to let the light from the streets in.

The street lights penetrated the room as the door swung open, followed by laughter, music and people shouting in the hall. The overhead intercom was blaring with doctors and other employees names being called.

"Would you excuse us for a minute. It'll be brief." Nurse Ashley and Jalise's conversation ceased as they faced Detective Morgan who was dressed in regular attire with a manila envelope in his hand.

"They can stay... I ain't got nothing for ya!" Willo shouted, freezing everyone in stride.

"You're right. This is yours... I'll be watching you." Detective Morgan said and tossed the envelope a few inches away from the wheelchair, and smiled.

Everyone watched the envelope land and Willo wheel towards it. Mr. James walked over and picked it up, handing it to Willo as a sudden knock sounded at the door.

"Come in, " Mr. James said as Willo opened the envelope with the nurses watching.

"What it do, fam," N.O shouted as he rushed towards Willo, smiling from ear to ear, paying little attention to Mr. James.

"Much love, bro!"

"United we be!"

"United we stand," Willo said after looking over the paper.

"I got E-bo with me. He in the car." N.O said.

The greeting had Mr. James and the nurses baffled as they listened. They eyed the paper Willo placed on his lap with concern.

"Pack this shit up! Let's roll! It's too many muthafucking police in this bitch! And they looking like a nigga a suspect or something. This ya bag too?" N.O said, looking at the plastic bag on the bed.

"Yes, Mr. James cut in, leaning over to get it as Nurse Jalise handed him a plastic bag and left with Nurse Ashley.

"This it? You gon need to clean this. Why they didn't clean the blood off this muthafucka for ya?" N.O said, looking inside the bag the nurse had handed him. He sat the bag in Willo's lap and started wheeling him towards the door.

"Mr. Malone, you can reach me at this number," Mr. James said, scribbling on a piece of paper as the room door was closing.

Unaware of Willo's real name, N.O was midway, between the elevator and room, in a conversation he was having both ways due to Willo's quietness and cold stare. Mr. James had caught N.O off guard, and it almost cost him his life.

"Malone," N.O spit out his mouth like venom as he aimed the Mini GlOCK .40 at Mr. James's abdominal area. "Go fluff some pillows, before your ass be needing one."

"Malone!"

The confrontation caused Willo to snap back to reality. "High Top... How can I?" He slung the paper at Mr. James, shocking N.O, who concealed the gun.

"Just pray," Mr. James responded, sounding assuring as he picked up the paper.

***

Standing on the back porch, Blot sipped on a Corona. The situation with Loco had him on edge. Ice's death was unexpected for him, and he hated it. Feeling the anger boiling up, he screamed to release the stress.

"Fuck," he yelled after turning up the bottle, draining it dry before slinging it into the darkness of the night.

***

Stunna greeted Peach as she opened the door with Mainlife and T-la indulged in small talk.

"Where she at, Peach," asked Stunna.

"I don't know... I took Moll Moll to the health clinic earlier. When we left, she was still sleeping." Peach replied as she stood to the side, letting them walk in.

"What's up, Peach," Mainlife spoke.

"Trying to make it. How you been, Mainlife?"

"I'm good. Where the ankle biter?"

"In the back, sleeping. Who is she?" Peach said, looking closely at T-la while closing the door.

"I'm T-la," she said to introduce herself.

"Family," Stunna shouted as he walked to the back.

"What happened to you? You want something to drink?"

"No thanks."

"I do."

"Mainlife, you know where the kitchen at."

"I had an accident," T-la told her as Mainlife walked off, making a call.

"Where you from, T-la," asked Peach, picking up the remote control, turning from a commercial to the six o'clock news.

"I stay behind Club Smokey's."

Chapter Fifteen

Peach turned the news down and leaned forward on the couch. "Which Smokey's?"

"On McDonough Boulevard across from Grant Street." T-la replied.

Peach got up with her nose turned up and left T-la lost and looking crazy.

Mainlife stood by Stunna, drinking a cup of Kool-Aid in Moll Moll's room, watching him sleep.

"Ebony know how the nigga look. She was fucking dude."

"Damn... Atlanta small as fuck. She know where dude at?"

"No. Safari punched her in the eye."

"She busting at Willo, and didn't shoot this mark. Mollie got snuffed over a bitch."

Bam!!!

Mainlife and Stunna jumped, hearing the door slam. They hurried out of the room, leaving Moll Moll sleeping with a stuffed dinosaur squished under his body.

"Where Peach," Stunna asked, seeing T-la staring at the TV.

"She went somewhere back there, and slammed the door. You ask me, the bitch got issues." T-la replied.

"What happened on the news, T," asked Mainlife.

"They talking bout the weather now."

"Did Peach say anything," Stunna asked concerned.

"She asked me where I was from, and I told her I stayed behind Club Smokey's. After that, she up and left." T-la recalled.

Stunna and Mainlife looked at each other, knowingly.

"Peach," Stunna yelled as he walked off.

"Yeah... You might want to check on her," T-la said nonchalantly. She felt her pockets as if making sure she was carrying.

"You better get right, T-la... Last time she did that, she whacked a nigga." Mainlife said as he walked over to the window and peeped out after hearing a car pulling in.

"I ain't tripping that. Where my phone? I know how to handle mines." T-la said sounding a little overconfident to Mainlife.

Stunna phones Sqizzle as he stood knocking on Peach's bedroom door. "Where bout you at?"

"I'm at the crib. I'll meet you at the spot later."

"Cool. I'm at Peach spot." Stunna said as he opened the door.

"T-la still with you," Peach voice came through the darkness of the room.

"Yeah, Peach," Stunna answered and turned on the room light.

"Tell her to answer her phone, bro," Sqizzle said, overhearing the conversation going on between Stunna and Peach.

"OK. Mom alright?"

"Yeah."

"OK. I'm on the way."

"Be safe, bro." Sqizzle ended the call.

Stunna stood, looking at Peach, who was curled up on the floor in fetus position, crying. "Peach, what's wrong with you?" He tried to help her up, but she refused, swinging and kicking at him wildly.

Peach sobbed and sniffed as she lay on the neon rug. Stunna made an attempt to help her again, and received a verbal demand.

"I want you to find him," she said in a voice that sounded nothing like hers.

Looking into her bloodshot eyes, Stunna understood her pain. "I will." He knelt down again, and this time, she gave in, hugging him tight as he lifted her from the floor and laid her on the bed. Her sobs enraged him.

Looking down, out of instinct, he noticed a picture on the floor where he'd picked Peach up from. His chest tightened as he looked at Mollie sitting on the hood of the Chevelle SS 396 with Peach standing between his legs, smiling from ear to ear in front of Club Smokey's. Not being able to take hearing her continue to cry, he placed the picture on the dresser and walked out the room speechless.

"That's you?" Stunna heard T-la ask Mainlife. He paid them no mind.

"Did she say anything about Mollie," Stunna asked stone faced, getting T-la and Mainlife's attention.

"Why would she," asked T-la.

"She's Mollie old lady," Mainlife responded before answering his phone.

"My bad... Nah. She was just like where I'm from, and I told her behind Club Smokey's."

"T-la, I'm gon need you to stay here for a minute."

"What?"

"Make sure Peach alright for me."

"You owe me," T-la said angrily. She wasn't the babysitting type.

Stunna walked off with Mainlife following in a reckless conversation. "As we ride, we die. Why you think they got bodies in the graveyard." Mainlife slammed the car door.

"Aye! Stunna!"

Mainlife and Stunna turned their heads in the direction of the voice to see two of Mechanicville's legends followed by a group walking towards the car.

"What up, Sam? Chris?" Stunna said as he nodded towards one of the men with a 30 Deep hoodie on.

"I'm glad I ran into you. I can't find nothing on this Mal nigga. Lil Noonie and Meat Meat laying low in University. They haven't heard shit. Big Greg and Scooby just left with Tonio And Lil Man to Pittsburgh.

"I got a new spot you need to check. A house from T-Ski and A.Z." Sammy Sam said, rubbing his beard.

"You don't got no more info on Mal," asked Big Chris before a fiend approached them.

"I just found out his name ain't Malcolm. It's Safari Malice." Stunna replied, watching as Mainlife answered his phone.

"Okay.. Okay.. That's why the nigga been off radar." Sammy Sam said.

"Hold up... Is this the same nigga Doug Jones looking for?" Big Chris interjected as the fiend hurried away happy as ever.

"There's a bag on his head," Sammy Sam said.

"Yup, he the same one," Mainlife responded.

"Safari Malice gamed," Big Chris said, nodding his head.

"I'm gamed too. I'm about to have the ups on his ass." Stunna said as he started the engine.

"Off his ass for the bread and for Mollie if I get to him first," Sammy Sam stated. He looked over his shoulder out of habit.

"We on it," Mainlife assured them as Stunna stomped on the gas pedal, making the Dual Flow Master's sound off.

***

"I don't know what to tell you, Danielle. It's a lot of shit fucked up. You know Ice wouldn't listen." Blot said while pacing back and forth in the living room.

"It's not right! It's not right! It's not right! Ice didn't deserve to die!" Danielle screamed hysterically.

"Get out of your feelings. He's dead, Danielle. No matter how much or long you sit around here bitching and complaining, the nigga ain't rising from the grave." Blot shot back as he held his head in despair. He walked off to cool his temper. *You're not the only one getting fucked behind the situation,* he thought to himself.

Chapter Sixteen

Hearing Danielle screaming, Blot knew Ice's death was taking its toll on her. Slamming the back door, he stood on the porch and dialed Juice's number.

"Whoa," answered Juice on the third ring.

"Where you at? I been trying to reach you."

"I'm good," Juice voice came in a slur as a car horn drowned out his speech.

"Where you at," Blot yelled into the receiver, trying to pinpoint his location.

"Uuuhhhh..." Juice grunted.

Baaaaaiiinnnggg!

"Juice! Juice! Juice!" Blot yelled over the blaring horn. Receiving no response, he hung up and ran down the porch steps to the Tahoe. He wasted no time - as he jumped in, he ignited the engine and drove off.

***

Stunna fumbled around in the console, trying to grab the phone as he drove down Grant Street.

***

Choke reassured the old man and woman with a sly look at his watch. "Clever just being Clever. He'll be here shortly. He's got another business meeting he's coming from. It's a new project; he been working off Buford Highway with Santiago Gomez... Have another drink."

Choke prayed silently that the Headless Horseman hurried. Knowing it's been an hour pass time, he tried not to grow impatient as he lit another Cuban Havana.

"I'm ready to go, baby... We've waited long enough. We're doing them a favor."

"Look... Mrs. Porter, Mr. Porter, he's going to show. You know how business gets tangled. We've done a lot for the both of you when y'all were overseas, like you asked us to. Let's enjoy ourselves. I promise you won't be disappointed."

"Uh... Boyd, when my wife is ready, she's ready. We've stayed beyond our intended stay. And as for business, I have more to tend to after this. So, we'll be ending this evening. Come on, luv."

Choke couldn't believe what he was hearing. He watched with unbelief radiating in his eyes as the couple eased out of the wraparound booth and started to leave. "Here comes drinks."

"More for you," Mrs. Porter turned halfway around and said, leaving Choke staring hard at their backs as they strutted to the exit.

Where y'all at, Choke thought as he stuck the cigar in a drink. He pushed the Chinese waitress, causing her to spill drinks. His action caused an uproar within the Dragon Yun Restaurant. The usually cheery dinner turned into an unpleasant night.

Choke was out the door before retaliation or the thought of someone throwing him out for the blatant disrespect. He noticed the

Headless Horseman's Lincoln Town Car pulling up at a creep. He climbed in his blood red Navigator truck and waited to see what he would do.

While observing, his phone's screen lit up on the dashboard. It was the Headless Horseman.

"I'm here... Where you parked at?"

"Put Clever on the phone," Choke demanded.

"Oooh... I see your truck." The Headless Horseman said, hanging up as a crowd of people poured out of the restaurant.

Choke seen the waitress and some other employees hurrying about as he looked through the rearview mirror, watching the Headless Horseman approach. The tension flared quickly as he opened the passenger door.

"Who you work for," Choke demanded to know as the Headless Horseman stepped up on the step rail.

"What you mean? I'm here."

"What the fuck you think? I told you to be here an hour ago. Get the fuck out, and follow me." Choke said harshly, shifting the gear to drive.

***

"Shots fired! Shots fired! Armed suspect fleeing, west on foot... Towards Confederate and Moreland Avenue... Armed suspect fleeing!" Detective Thomas's dashboard crackled to life as he was parked in the parking lot of the gentlemen's club, Foxy Lady.

He radioed for back and started the unmark Crown Victoria. He scanned the parking lot, looking at every black male who entered the club the last three hours. Taping the picture of the suspect to the dashboard, he gunned down the street, heading for the action.

It was a lively night out. Detective Thomas weaved through traffic while hyping himself up by continuing to repeat *protect and serve by any means,* in his mind. Being minutes away from the dispatched call didn't stop him from pushing the vehicle to its limits.

***

"Ohhh! Shit! Willo!" Mainlife yelled, answering the phone as Stunna turned on Hay Good Avenue, going down the back streets.

***

"Here... Here go some clean towels. Your father want to see you this weekend."

"What time we going," Sqizzle asked his mother, turning off the shower.

"He just want you to come," she replied and closed the door.

Sqizzle dried off, thinking. He knew when his father wanted a one on one visit, something was up. Looking in the mirror, he stared hard until he seen his face behind the pupils he was looking in. His dark skin complexion darkened as he thought about Mollie.

***

Choke mumbled, watching the road as the Headless Horseman tailed him. *Crumbling. Crumbling.* He thought, not understanding why Mr. Porter would downplay him after all the years of his and Clever's loyal services. Even though it was Clever who introduced them, he felt Mr. Porter was obligated to conduct business with him when summoned.

How could Mr. Porter be so blind, Choke thought, thinking about the proposal. He was the muscle; Clever was the brain of the operation. But, the idea was gift wrapped. The income would be profitable for all. Now, it was only a fading dream.

***

"We turning on Hill Street now. Get yourself straight. We gon slide through. Got the name of dude who shot your spot up." Mainlife spoke in the receiver, excited as Stunna drove down the dark back street.

***

"What happened right here?"

Juice enjoyed the feeling of the feminine touch, tracing the outline of the scar on his chest. Relaxed from smoking some upscale marijuana and after great sex, he lay in the king size at the Ramada Inn. The woman's soothing voice and almond butter colored body worked miracles for him. The long hours of erotic sex had him exhausted, which he loved, because it allowed him to escape the reality of his lifestyle.

***

Safari Malice danced through Stunna's mind as he passed under the blinking street light.

Plan

Chapter Seventeen

A crowd of people was gathered at the intersection of Hill Street and Nolan Avenue, gambling on the corner. Stunna slowed down as he was being flagged down. With Safari Malice on his mind, he didn't feel like shooting the breeze or kicking it. He observed the area, seeing the dice game was full throttle in front of a burnt orange Delta 88's headlights.

The life of the streets wouldn't let Stunna cruise on by. K-Thumper jumped out in front of the Cutlass. "Put down, lil nigga! I know you got it on ya!" K-Thumper shook his closed right fist, making sure Stunna could hear the clanking sound of the two dice.

"I can't O.G. I'm on the move."

"Fuck nah! Y'all gotta pull over! K-Thumper, come roll the dice, nigga!" An NFL linebacker size man yelled with a half full Grey Goose bottle in his left hand.

"Slow up, Perm! I'm trying to get these niggas to break bread!" K-Thumper said, redirecting the conversation as Perm turned the bottle up. Music boomed from the corner house as if it was a house party going on.

"Nah, we good. I gotta catch up with the nigga who killed Mollie."

"Yeah. I told Mainlife we'll go to war with ya."

"I told him," Mainlife spoke up. "We got the name of the mark now. Safari Malice. Dude be moving around swiftly."

"Let us know what's good then, yung. What side of town he from?"

"I'm on my way to see what the move is now," Stunna replied.

"Shit... We can mount up now. What's up?" K-Thumper said as he rolled the dice.

"Man! What the fuck!" Perm and four other guys yelled as K-Thumper bucked his point and threw the dice afterwards.

"It's time to ride! They found the nigga who killed Mollie. Aye! Bang!" K-Thumper yelled towards the corner house.

***

The residential neighborhood was far from the projects Choke grew up in. Passing the Governor's Mansion, driving the speed limit with caution on Paces Ferry Road, Choke killed the lights and eased off the road. Business was work, and work was a job. Ever since Archibald and Rudy questioned his loyalty, he'd been scoping out Keith's location.

Choke texted the Headless Horseman. *Stay in the car. Make sure Clever don't try any stunts.* He hopped out of the truck and walked along the manicured treeline, creeping low like a panther on the prowl.

The brick Badgley Mischka structured home looked like a dream house from West Hollywood with the groundwork glowing a dull blue and yellow lighting as it did around the landscape.

It was now or never, as Choke peeped his head from around the side of a parked Cadillac Escalade ESV Edition that was gloss black. He made it to the side door of the house, growling internally at his prey.

The kitchen light was dim with candles lit around the edge of a glass work island. Soft jazz played throughout the house.

B. B King's The Thrill Is Gone played in Choke's mind as he slithered along with snake like instincts. The sounds of moaning and groaning quickly pierced his ears, causing him to slow down, as he eased pass a custom made library. Approaching the partly opened sliding door with lion head knobs, the intimate sounds became louder. He eased towards the door with caution, looking for the unexpected.

Gun in hand and ready to scratch another problem off his to do list, Choke bust in the room and opened fire.

***

After relieving himself, Juice stared down at the naked woman laying in the bed and grabbed his crotch. Walking over to the window, he peered out the blinders at the parking lot as his phone started ringing. Avoiding the call, he closed the blinders and held his erect manhood while walking back towards the woman on the bed.

***

"Ebony know how the mark look and everything. That means she knows how to find him too." Mainlife said, returning from the kitchen with a garbage bag hanging from his back pocket as he carried a brown box.

"I can't wait to snatch his ass up," Stunna said with the phone held to his ear, counting money.

"She still ain't answer," Mainlife asked, dropping the box on a foldable table.

"Hell nah," Stunna replied while dialing Co Kizzy number as he got up and paced the floor.

"We gon catch this fool before the year drop... Look, this that shark food. Bro came through on this. This shit strong." Mainlife said, examining the substance in the box.

"What kinda weed is that," Stunna asked, sniffing the air.

"Sharklato. Sharks gotta eat. Niggas gon love this."

Knock! Knock! Knock! The banging on the door got their attention. The back door was rattling as Stunna made his way to it.

Knock! Knock! Knock!

***

"Blot calling again," Man yelled to Hot, eyeing his phone as he was sacking marijuana up.

"I don't got no talk for that nigga," Hot hollered back.

"We need to cash his ass in," Man suggested as voicemail popped up on the screen.

"That nigga broke! This weed is all he had! Him and Juice. I'm surprised we struck this good. It's good we waited like Rack said."

"Where Rack put the dope?"

"To make a play, he better," Hot said, walking up in an all red Dickie suit with Brat-Lyfe spray painted on it, brushing his waves.

"Who you think dude was?"

"Who," Hot asked, breaking down the buds.

"Dude from Doug spot... I still be thinking bout him."

"I don't see why. The nigga dead. I'm glad we murked Ice. Had us on a goof trip, carrying that nigga. Where they get this weed from?" Hot said with excitement.

"I don't know, but we bout to set Cleveland on fye. I'm gon five for twenties these niggas."

"I'm gon open shop in K-Mart."

"Who that?"

Man looked over at his phone at the contact name, and nodded with a smirk. "Blot."

"Watch this," Hot said and answered the phone as Man got up to answer the knock at the door with gun in hand.

Man opened the door to a mean mugging and scarred face York. "What you want?"

"Yo sun... Shorty pointed me here. I'm trying to smoke. You got their Diesel?"

Man looked up and down the walkway, making mental notes of the people who were posted and walking around. "I got some Cush."

***

"It's not that simple..." Keith's Barry White baritone voice froze Choke in place. The unexpected reversed to the expected waiting in the dark.

Chapter Eighteen

Choke was speechless as he was looking from the wall projecting porn movie around the room for Keith. Darkness. Keith cut the power off, causing Choke's eyes to see white specks as he aimed at nothing. He came to realize Keith wasn't just a black Pee Wee Herman, but a snake as well.

"Looks can be deceiving, he thought while trying to focus on Keith's movements.

"On the outside looking in. Tell me, how do you feel?"

"Show your face, Keith!"

The room was deathly silent. Fear, surprise, anger. Transformation fogged the atmosphere with the ultimate unexpected neither expected. The sound was alarming to Choke's ears as he sidestepped, hearing the bullet enter the chamber.

"You know my name!" The lights immediately came on, blinding Choke.

Blah! Blah! Blah! Choke let off three rounds blindly, thinking to buy himself time to refocus. "You going to know mines too, but in Hell."

"You right," Keith said as he turned the lights out again from his secret location.

Raqa! Raqa!

Thud! Choke tripped over an unidentified object, causing pain to shoot up his right leg. He bit his tongue and closed his eyes in an attempt to subside the pain.

"Stupid, boy," Keith said.

Choke scrambled to his feet, gripping the gun tighter, looking in the direction he could only assume he'd find Keith.

Blah! Blah!

"Fool, use all your bullets. I got something for you." Keith's voice danced in Choke's ears, causing him to spin, letting off more shots.

Blah! Blah! Blah!

***

The Headless Horseman snapped his head around as he was standing over a rosebush, urinating at the ringing of his phone. He had to force himself to cut his bathroom break short. In doing so, he found himself showering his shoes.

"Yeah," he answered the phone, anticipating Choke's next order of instructions. But it ended up being a shock. Seeing the name on the caller's ID, he frowned. The voice wasn't to his liking, but he knew it well.

The Headless Horseman nodded to the request of another connect, and ended the call. He placed the phone back in the cupholder and stared at the path Choke had disappeared down.

***

Blot was two wheeling the Tahoe, driving fast with several busted nerves after listening to Hot. Driving through Fulton County, violating the speed limit, he was zoned out, listening to Wacka Flocka, running red lights and stop signs as the song Hard In The Paint boomed through the speakers. A long day had become an even longer night was his thoughts. The Christmas spirit had most of Atlanta smiling without any knowledge of anything unpleasant as the unfortunate and lowlife were trapped in a world of their own.

Eeeeeerve! Cllllsssshhh! Blot stomped on the brakes with both feet, causing all four wheels to lock up. Police cars were everywhere up ahead near Cleveland Avenue as he came up on Old Hapeville Road from Macon Drive. Quick thinking, he hit reverse and headed back down Macon Drive. Watching through the side mirror, he felt the tension ease knowing he wasn't being pursued.

Passing Cleveland Park, Christmas lights were flashing on every rooftop, poster and doorpost. It was the least thing on Blot's mind as he drove to put distance between him and the scene he almost ran head first into.

***

"Damn, bro... I forgot to tell her. She still over Peach." Stunna told Sqizzle as he returned from the kitchen, phone in hand and looking around. Picking up a bottle of Hennessey off the table, he walked towards the front window, drinking. Peering out at the night, he sorted through his thoughts as Sqizzle and Mainlife loaded clip after clip.

"Stunna," Mainlife yelled, jumping up out the chair, knocking over his cup of Hennessey.

Blah! Blah! Blah!

"Ohh... Shit! Shoot that nigga!" Sqizzle said as he jumped up.

***

"Knowing person name doesn't mean shit if you don't know the person. Ahhh! Yaaahh!" The contact of Keith's heel caused Choke to collapse instantly. He'd caught him with a swift spinning heel kick to the face. Taking off the night vision goggles, Keith stepped over Choke's twisted body and walked off. Flipping the light switch to on, he spotted Choke's gun.

Choke mustered up enough strength to get back to his feet. Staggering, he held the left side of his face. He was regaining some sense of composure, but everything was still blurry.

"Nah... It won't be none of that." Before Choke could readjust, Keith met him with a Floyd Mayweather knockout blow to the chin. The unexpected was unexpected.

Choke was airborne from the right hook, seeing stars and everything else that came with the force.

Thud!

Satisfied, Keith scanned the room. Choke lay stretched out in front of a half inflated blowup doll with grease all over her. Rushing off barefooted and in boxers and oily, Keith smiled with a thought.

***

"Well, it's nice to see you on short notice, Mr. Porter and the lovely Mrs. Porter," Str 1 said as they were standing outside of Hooters downtown Underground.

"Hey, don't get fly with my lady. You know how I am about her." Mr. Porter said, pulling his wife into a passionate kiss.

"He can't walk in your shoes, baby," Mrs. Porter commented.

"It's the holidays. You know I don't mean no harm." Str 1 said apologetically.

"You're right. So, this going to be short and brief too. Now, if it's about funding your record label, it's a no... Straight One, I told you, I don't know nothing about the music business."

"Mr. Porter, it's not about knowing. You know people though, and that's what count." Str 1 replied, stepping closer as people started walking by.

A smile came upon Mr. Porter's face. Knowing his position and the circle of people he interacted with, he understood the influence Str 1 spoke of.

"I have to go to the restroom," Mrs. Porter whispered to her husband.

"Okay, bae... I know a lot of people. But, it's no good if I don't know what I'm investing in. I'm held accountable for my money, and she's my accountant. I invest in profitable business. Real estate, car lots... You need to invest in cars, since you stay in a different one every time we meet. How about managing one of my lots? Top of the line Chevrolets.

"Ask Kevin Hardwick... I own ten Chevy car lots. Lance Nathaniel Triplett Boulevard is where I first started. You won't ever have to buy a car again."

"I'm not into managing no cars. I do music, you know that. Music is what I breathe. Mr. Porter, the artists I manage are going to blow up like T.I or Young Jeezy. We can turn Atlanta upside down, trust me. I know you heard my newest artist, Dirty Life?"

We'll See

Chapter Nineteen

Hooters was in full holiday swing as Mrs. Porter semi partied her way to the restroom around the college crowd. Str 1 stared and listened, rubbing his face as Mr. Porter ranted.

"Listen... I can turn you into a millionaire. This year, I made 3.5 million off selling cars alone. I own Lance Nathaniel Triplett Boulevard. Do you want to do business?" Mr. Porter said with a stern look.

"I'm not no car salesman. I'm a music producer. My artists are the next best thing going."

"Well... Think about it.. Call me when you have."

"I came to seal a deal."

"Yeah... Think about it. Get back with me in a week or two. My night still young." Mr. Porter said, winking towards Hooters entrance.

"You serious?"

He nodded, and Str 1 understood. Str 1 left Mr. Porter standing with his hand held out with a smirk on his face. Standing and smirking, Mr. Porter watched the backs of every person who passed him as he waited for Mrs. Porter to return. Seeing Str 1's taillights disappear in the distance, he strolled inside of Hooters.

***

"That was a big ass rat," Sqizzle said, uncaging Kujo and Sheba while looking at the crack in the bottom of the kitchen door.

"The little fucker was fast. I tried to stiff the nigga. Look at the holes in the wall." Mainlife said, reloading as he stood next to the refrigerator.

"Something ain't right," Stunna said cautiously after peeping the commotion.

"What," Mainlife questioned, looking from Sqizzle to Stunna.

"Ebony."

"Stunna, we don't need her. On the land, we gon find Safari Malice. Let's go catch up with Willo. As long as I'm breathing, we friends to the end. Fuck that - we brothers. Ain't that right, Sqizzle?" Mainlife knew Stunna wouldn't rest on an open promise, knowing Mollie was looking down on him.

Sqizzle was on edge and wanting to dive off at first sight of Safari Malice. "Yeah." He answered his phone, seeing York's name on caller's ID.

"Ebony know how the nigga look. I got to get at her."

"You bailed her ass out. She better call." Sqizzle yelled. He pulled the hoodie over his head and hurried towards the door.

"Where you going," Stunna demanded to know.

"Meet up with York."

***

The scent of gasoline was unbearable. Choke pulled the tip of his shirt over his nose, staggering to his feet. The opened room door was a breath of fresh air entering his lungs without having walked through it yet. On wobbly legs, dizzy and angry, he walked towards the door.

Time wasn't time. Choke didn't care about time. He stumbled along, face still in pain, and shoeless.

"Ohhh! You didn't think it'll be that easy, did you? See, you street niggas are dumb as you look. But, I take you as a old street nigga. Early 40s. You're standing in gas by the way.."

Fear crept through his body upon hearing the truth of his current situation that Keith spoke nonchalantly.

"I got full coverage house insurance, that comes with a damn good fireproof guarantee return," Keith boasted as he revealed his whereabouts.

Seeing Keith step from behind the China cabinet he'd spit on earlier, Choke felt as illiterate as Keith had called him. He had the feeling as if standing on a landmine, knowing he stood on a gasoline soaked carpet and seeing the red cherry of the cigarette Keith had dangling between his lips.

***

"Freeze! Freeze! Get down! Now! Get down!"

Flashlights were strobing spontaneously as officers adrenaline rushed. Mainlife and Stunna came out the house, puzzled. It hadn't been twenty minutes, since Sqizzle left them. Guns were drawn and aimed at them.

Police cruisers and unmarked Sedans crisscrosses the street, doubled parked. The moon was full and high up, shining bright enough to see everyone clearly. Grant Street looked like the Grand Opera on Broadway, but with an urban twist.

***

Pulling up in the exotic Dream Girl parking lot, Blot spotted Man and Hot sitting on the hood of a black 72 Chevy Malibu, drinking with a female. Swerving the Tahoe hard, he jumped out in front of them, leaving the door open. "Aye bitch, get the fuck on! What the fuck? I been calling y'all niggas for a reason! You can't hear?" He didn't leave any room for open end conversation. The female was stunned and so were Man and Hot.

"Move bitch," Blot growled, getting the reaction he wanted.

"Nigga, you tripping. You don't know what we been going through, so slow the fuck down." Man said, hopping off the hood, getting up in Blot's face. The female hurried up and left.

"Yeah, slow down." Hot sided with Man.

"Nah, fuck that! I'm here... What business y'all got going on here, Hot? Nothing, I can see.

"These hoes can wait! I been blowing y'all niggas up since yesterday. Y'all don't got time to be kicking the lil boy shit! Somebody smoked Ice and Dig. Y'all niggas signed on to this shit. So, what's up?" Blot yelled, staring both men down.

Man and Hot looked at each other and nodded.

"Don't get it twisted," Hot said as he grabbed the bottle of Hennessey off the roof of the car.

"For real, for real," Man agreed, easing his hand from under his shirt.

"Twisted," Blot frowned, feeling his adrenaline starting to pump.

Vvvrrroooom... Vvvrrroooom... Vvvrrroooom...

A group of Kawasaki Ninjas broke the budding tension as they came ruff riding in the parking lot. The riders turned the parking lot into a Daytona dragstrip. Burning out, they had the parking lot smoky and vibrating. Neither man spoke a word as they watched several security guards rush the bikers.

***

The Headless Horseman was in a full throttle conversation with himself. His dual personality was starting to blend into one. "What? Who? Fuck!"

The fleeing Cadillac Escalade got his attention as it recklessly sped its way out the driveway, cartwheeling onto Paces Ferry Road, tail lighting away. The Headless Horseman eyed the path he'd remember seeing Choke disappear down, thinking. The treeline had him secluded and baffled. He pocketed the phone and jumped out the car with his gun in reach and ready.

Seconds within the treeline, he stopped in his tracks and looked over his right shoulder, hearing a loud motor of some sort. The sound swooshed pass with a twirling orange light trailing. The scent of scorched wood and plastic had the Headless Horseman's nose twitching as he headed deeper down the path.

***

"Eat.. My cousin didn't save you for nothing. You owe him. I don't know what they got planned for you, but you better regain your strength." Danielle's Nia Long beauty faded to a look of a jaded sunflower.

Safari Malice struggled with painful moans as she forced back tears. Trapped in a hustler's nightmare, he was awake and living it.

Chapter Twenty

Danielle watched Safari Malice as he sipped the Ensure through a Capri Sun's straw. She noticed the blood seeping through the bandages. Knowing what she had to do, she clinched her jaws and exhaled.

"I want to know your name? Ice said it's a reason you're missing a thumb. I took you in because of Ice... Now, he's dead... I can't say it's because of you because I know my cousin wasn't no saint... Who am I saving? Juice wanna kill you."

She knelt before him, watching his eyelids for a reaction. It was no use due to the swelling and bruises around the eyes. Danielle's heart was crying out sincerely as she anticipated him say his name.

Beaten beyond recognition, Safari Malice tried to reach out. Danielle snatched the pillow off his lap, causing Ensure everywhere.

"Tell me your name? You owe Ice..."

Safari Malice's lips quivered. His eyelids began to flutter.

"Who are you? Where your family?"

The questions worked a nerve. Partially opening the right eye revealed a crimson red bloodshot eyeball. A purplish tear streaked down his cheek as he forced the eye opened, causing her flesh to crawl with goosebumps. The purplish, reddish tear had her speechless.

"Aaaahhh..." He managed to get out. His lips trembled as he struggled with the burning sensation of pain, trying to speak.

"Tell me," Danielle demanded through tearstained eyes.

"Ssss aaa hh..." He gasped uncontrollably and began coughing up blood.

"Wait... Wait... Wait..." Danielle jumped up with reflexes like a cat, bracing his body before his head hit the floor. Agony and pain was etched into his body's movement and facial expression.

***

"What the fuck!" The Headless Horseman couldn't believe his eyes as they teared up. Fumes and flames had him coughing and squinting as he made his way towards the back of the burning house. The crackling sound of burning wood stopped him in mid stride, causing him to look over his left shoulder towards a shed.

Observing nothing other than a torched house, the Headless Horseman pulled the phone out and dialed Choke. "Choke, where you at?" All he could hear is, music in the receiver. He approached the open door with caution.

Boooom!

***

Officer David sat, waiting for his turn to interrogate the young suspect. He noticed Detective Thomas was getting short winded.

"He robbed a liquor store. You say his name is Mainlife, right?" Detective Thomas said, writing in a notepad.

"I told you... Is y'all listening? How much my bond?"

"Harvey, answer my question. This guy is wanted for some shootings two weeks ago... You do know, you're telling me about another incident, in which I can charge him for since you know he robbed a liquor store?"

"I didn't say it like that... I said his name Mainlife. Where my bond?"

"You're not getting a bond if you don't give us what we want, smart ass. I'm not gonna take it easy on your ass like Detective Thomas. See, the people house you broke in... Remember, you had a gun when you robbed them? Harvey, you're in a world of trouble if you don't start talking."

"I didn't have no gun," Harvey replied, puffing his chest up.

"Shut the hell up! I didn't ask you to speak! You see this badge? It say Officer David! Me! When Detective Thomas was speaking, that was your time to spill!" Officer David paced around the room like a lion stalking its prey as Harvey protested.

"I... I... I just took some TVs. Y'all got them out the car. I didn't have no gun! They lying!"

"I guess you were too high to remember the robbing spree! For what you're in here for! And that stolen car you were in, it was used in a double homicide... Isn't that right, Detective Thomas?"

Detective Thomas was hesitant as he observed Officer David's tactics. The interrogation had a light of its own that was very dark in Harvey's eyes. He couldn't believe what he was hearing.

"I didn't kill nobody! I want to go home! Y'all got me for theft."

"The Department of Corrections is about to be your new home. Double homicide carries 2 life sentences... Plus, your arm robberies, that's another 50 years without parole."

"Man, you tripping! I didn't rob or kill nobody!"

"He's right, Mr. Harvey. The car been on the lookout list, and your fingerprints are all over it. I can't say you're the killer because I wasn't there. But you're definitely a suspect now."

"Detective Thomas, nah! I didn't kill nobody. I'm telling you the truth."

"You telling the truth? Now, that's a good one. You hear that, Detective Thomas? He's telling the truth. A life sentence isn't a light sentence. 2 life sentences isn't enough for your dumb ass. I'm gonna make sure the Judge Hicks deny your bond, so get catching flight out ya head."

"It'll be up to the DA if you're telling the truth. If you are, then you have nothing to worry about."

"I didn't do anything!"

"Fuck that crying! You do the crime, you do the time! You want to rob and kill people? Two officers were injured in your attempt to flee and allude, so you going down.

"This name better be accurate. Do you know where we can find him?" Officer David growled at Harvey. Detective Thomas stood in the corner with arms folded across his chest.

"I don't know where he be at. I wanna go home! I didn't rob nobody. They owed me, so I got some TVs." Harvey rocked back and forth in the steel chair.

"You lying! You robbed them! How come you don't know where he be? You don't know a person name just by knowing it. Have you seen him before?"

"I seen him around. That's about it."

"In what area," Detective Thomas asked as he walked around the chair, knowing his action made Harvey feel that much more uncomfortable.

"I can't recall, but I seen him."

"Now, look you piece of shit... You better come up with a location. Where you got the name from?" Officer David shouted.

Harvey felt as though he was shrinking under the Officer David's bombardment of questions.

"He's right, Harvey. It's no way y'all know a name just by a mere glimpse. If you wanna go home, act like it. Do you know this man?" Detective Thomas said, holding up a photocopy picture.

"I... I... I... I..."

"I. I. I my ass! You need a speech therapist? I'll help you talk." Officer David growled and grabbed Harvey by the collar.

"No.. No, I don't know him. I seen him around... In a club or somewhere." Harvey replied, looking at the picture.

"That's not enough. Charge his ass, Detective Thomas. We have our suspect right here."

"No! No! I didn't kill nobody! Honestly! I'm telling the truth!"

"How do you know him? And where is he from?" Officer David yelled.

"He.. He.. He go with a girl I know. He from, from Gra, Grant Street."

www.ingramcontent.com/pod-product-compliance
Lightning Source LLC
Chambersburg PA
CBHW020559160726
47991CB00002B/789